Dark Circles

A collection of short stories and poems

Dark Circles

A collection of short stories and poems

Fresher Publishing

Copy Editor: Katie Havicon
Marketing Lead: Sarah Rees
Digital Editor: Mohammed Ahmed
Designer/Art Editor: Mariela Casanova

Dark Circles

A collection of short stories and poems

A Bournemouth Writing Prize anthology
First published 2022 by Fresher Publishing

Fresher Publishing
Bournemouth University
Weymouth House
Fern Barrow
Poole
Dorset BH12 5BB

www.fresherpublishing.co.uk
email bournemouthwritingprize2022@bournemouth.ac.uk

Cover designed by: Mariela Casanova

Contents

Acknowledgements

Bournemouth University, home of Fresher Publishing, brings the voices and visions of great writers to you, the reader. This would not have been possible without the unfaltering expertise, support and enthusiasm of our lead tutor, Emma Scattergood. We are also hugely indebted to the guidance on design given by Saeed Rashid, and to Ed Peppitt for his skilled assistance in creating the digital product. To our fellow students with whom we enjoyed working during the copy-editing stages, we extend our thanks.

It has been our privilege to bring these remarkable works of fiction and poetry to life for distribution to a global audience. From the initial reading of the entries, through to the selection of our favourites for inclusion in this book, we have been delighted by the imagination and narrative style of the writers who have contributed. Thank you to all our talented authors.

It's been a long journey from the authors who wrote each piece to the moment you hold this compilation. After all the hard work, we are pleased to release this publication for everyone to dive into! We thank you, the reader, for picking up *Dark Circles* and we hope you enjoy reading the stories as much as we did compiling them.

The editorial team

Foreword

Welcome to *Dark Circles*, an anthology of tales (and people) that take risks. From stalkers to mafia bosses to cigarette sellers, this book takes you into the psyches of those who would trade your life for theirs, reflecting ideals and desires that most of us would never dare hold too close to the light.

These dark stories of murder and crime suggest new ways of seeing ourselves, and our place in the world, and are guaranteed to keep you turning pages late into the night. Each one was carefully selected from submissions to the Bournemouth Writing Prize by us, a small editorial team of students on the MA Creative Writing & Publishing course at Bournemouth University. Below, we offer some thoughts on our favourite stories and poems. (Warning – you may find yourself sleeping with the lights on...)

Katie: What I love about reading fiction is the disarming feeling of being removed from your own reality and finding yourself – often piece by piece as the story unfolds – in a different world. My subversive side enjoys quirkiness, so 'Accurate to One-Sixteenth of an Ounce' appealed to me straight away. Being a dog-lover, I was gripped by the plight of the innocents in this hauntingly strange but eerily convincing tale of retribution.

Sarah: Crime fiction is one of my guilty pleasures, so this job has been such a pleasure for me, making it impossible to select just one favourite. Every story highlights the darkness lurking in the human soul, but each offers a different perspective. You will hear from both victims and perpetrators and find yourself empathising with some surprising characters!

Ahmed: I have always held a love for thrillers and, during the making of this anthology, was so impressed with the sensational stories. Like Sarah, I find it difficult to choose only one story as my favourite.

Mariela: My interest in crime and justice stories began in my teens, so working on this collection was an absolute pleasure. All short stories in this book are gripping. Still, I would like to point out two poems: 'Hecuba', which deals gently with domestic violence and considers murder as revenge, or perhaps just a desire for divine justice. A second piece, 'Bogeyman', depicts an adult reflecting on childhood trauma caused by an evil figure or, more precisely, portraying an abuser who meets his end.

The editors

Hecuba

By Kenneth Hickey

Kenneth Hickey was born in 1975 in Cobh, Co. Cork Ireland. He served in the Irish Naval Service between 1993 and 2000. His poetry and prose has been published in various literary journals in Ireland, the UK and the United States including Southword, Crannoig, THE SHOp, A New Ulster, Aesthetica Magazine and The Great American Poetry show. His writing for theatre has been performed in Ireland, the UK, New York and Paris. He has won the Eamon Keane Full Length Play Award as well as being shortlisted for The PJ O'Connor Award and the Tony Doyle Bursary. His work in film has been screened at the Cork and Foyle Film Festivals. He holds a BA and MA in English Literature both from University College Cork. His debut collection 'The Unicycle Paradox' was published by Revival Press in November 2021. He still resides in Cork.
www.kenhickeypoetry.wordpress.com

Men's lawless lusts are all called love

She sits alone in the cool grey dawn
At the fractured make-up mirror
Hiding the work of his heavy hand
In the silence of sleeping children's dreams.

The cyclops breathes heavily on the bed
Devourer of sweetest human flesh
Guarding all approaches to this high tower
No helmeted knight rides from Camelot.

She whispers low to the virgin mother
Only fragile panting prayers remain
In time there will be flowers; muted apologies
The earth rights on its axis again.

Till savage beast unmasks once more
Beating bright beauty to the unwashed floor.

She fixes her smile; continues to weep
And waits for the man to die in his sleep.

Burgerflippers

By Jeffrey Robertson

Jeffrey Robertson worked for the Australian Government in the field of foreign policy and North Asia, focusing on China, the Korean Peninsula and Japan. Now he writes from the other side of the line – as an academic, consultant, sometimes spy fiction ghost writer, and always aspiring fiction author. His research, writing, commentary, and contact details can be found online at https://junotane.com.

There were five judges. The second judge was an employee of the publisher. She was a senior editor with a retinue of well-known authors working with her. The third judge was an employee of the sponsor – a senior employee. He had no interest in literature, but knew that young writers often drank too much, and in his words, were just as often caught by the chance of escaping writing to be with a banker. The fourth judge was a stern, no nonsense literary agent. She'd remind you of the school librarian if you were, like younger me, annoyed by dark libraries when the sun shone and birds sang, begging you to climb trees to look at their nest. The fifth judge needs no introduction. Pinkie Ong was the author of three now well-known novels: *Blurred Borders*, *Confusion*, and *The Ghost Writer*. No, I haven't mentioned the first judge. We'll discuss him later. The judges of the Penn Paris Fiction Prize awaited our briefing in the consultation room.

Quite frankly, I didn't see any threat. Now, I know nothing about fiction or literature – and come to think of it, I'm not even sure whether those two things are the same or not. Nevertheless, I was responsible for reassuring them, the Chief Inspector said.

'Protect them from what?' I was asked by Kassim in the tea room.

'I mean, it's a bloody story!' Hancock joined in. She thought the idea was absurd, 'Are you going to write a detective story to catch the writer?' She was right; it was absurd.

It all started two weeks after the competition closed. There were twenty grad students assigned to read the short stories. That surprised me in the first instance, but the organizers assured me it was normal. Each entry cost twenty dollars, the prize was $5,000. They expected, or rather needed, at least 250 to break even. With a $5,000 prize and entry open across the globe, they expected around 3,000 entries, and had received 3,689. That provided more than enough money to pay the prize, run the website and promotions, honorariums, and expenses for the judges, and pay minimum wage to twenty grad students.

All the grad students had to do was create two piles: stories they liked, and stories they disliked. The judges would then get to work and read the stories which passed the grad student culling. Simple as could be. But four of the grad students ended up with a third pile – stories that concerned them. Each grad student who created that pile, had only one story in the pile.

Two of them were actually in the same room when it occurred. They had that 'Oh fuck' moment at the same time. The moment when you realize the urgency of a situation. They were across from each other in the reading room – a room prepared in the publisher's office, provided with snacks and an endless supply of black coffee. They were dead bored with reading story after story (they later told me most stories only required the first paragraph to rid themselves of it). In the midst of that boredom, they started reading the story, looked around, confused and scared, and caught each other's eyes. The first words of one was, 'What the...', and the other simply mouthed what she was thinking, 'Fffffaaa...'. The first called the others to the table and asked them to read it, the second realized it was the same story, and it went on from there.

The competition organizers brought it up the chain of command. Each of the judges read the story. Despite the publisher and the sponsor trying to calm them, each wanted it dealt with. And given their collective weight, not in pounds but in connections, that was why the judges awaited our briefing in the consultation room.

Our own budding writer, DC Cleaver, the college boy,

reckoned the whole thing was a ruse. Detectives are always suspicious, and we all have an annoying desire to convince everyone else. 'It's perfect! Look, who gives an ass about a short story competition?' He looked across at Bunson. Fat old Bunson, eating as always. He was a comic book copper. Overweight, ill-fitting suit, his desk full of papers – I swear he wrote emails on paper before he sent them online – and an ever-present donut and black coffee within reach. Cleaver walked over, grabbed a donut from Bunson's six-pack donut box. 'When's the last time you read a story Bunson?' Bunson looked annoyed, mumbled something, smiled, then moved the donut box behind his bowling ball case. Cleaver continued, 'You see, the daily news won't report on a story competition, add in a threat like this, and you've got the front page – easy.' He made sense. 'I'll give you odds, it's the organizers themselves – I mean, it's just a bloody story.'

Everyone was pretty pissed off. The last week had been exhausting. We tracked down, followed and observed one Ernst Stammers – the only suspect spat out by headquarters computers. Ernst Stammers was a mystery in himself. He started out in Paris as a budding writer, gave up writing and ended up as an adjunct professor in Seoul, South Korea. He was known to have mental health issues, which started as an unhealthy obsession and then paranoia concerning North Korea. He had a breakdown, then disappeared off the radar. He turned up in Paris a few years ago. Turns out he was trying to 'restart' his writing career that never really started by following and harassing Pinkie Ong. She took out a restraining order and he again disappeared off the radar. That's what linked him to the current case.

When we got to Paris, the locals had him under observation at 'Le Tambour' – a 24-hour café on Rue

Montmartre, catering to the butchers and bakers in the early morning, the delivery drivers of a mid-morning, the post office crowd at lunch, and the lazy stragglers from local bars after they closed. They'd arrested him only last month banging on the windows of a venue just a few doors up the road apparently wanting to be let in for a 'pint after hours', which, when the French police said it, sounded funnier than when I told the Chief Inspector.

Bunson and I worked with the locals, who put six officers on the case. We tracked Ernst Stammers for three days.

On the first day, we received an update that he'd moved north from 'Le Tambour', heading towards Rue Saint-Denis. This was considered significant because it would bring him to the sad remnants of a once thriving red light district. Ernst Stammers managed to capture all of its sadness, his age, and his senility by entering a premises splashed in red with the English language title, 'Sexy Red Center Projection DVD'. One of the younger officers mentioned he had no clue what a DVD actually was, so we sent him in with Bunson for educational purposes. Ernst Stammers was asleep in a booth watching a DVD. The madame agreed to call when he left. We sat in a pizza restaurant nearby and waited. The call came later that evening that he'd left. The video and receipts from inside the Sexy Red Center were procured. He watched porn and intermittently wrote in his notebook. He purchased a *poupée en rose* – a pink sex doll. He carried it with him, not yet inflated, I'll add, to 'Le Tambour'.

The second day he headed to the west. Ernst Stammers was tracked to the Jardin des Tuileries, where he sat dead center of its largest expanse of green grass. I say green as if it could be any other color. Perhaps brown, if dry? Nevertheless, it was green. For an entire day it was the same. He sat on the grass, moved to a bench, sat on the grass again. He was reading a book and occasionally writing in his notebook. The book was in Russian – an officer passed the imagery to headquarters where it was translated – *The Big Green Tent* by Lyudmila Ulitskaya. This meant nothing to me. At 4.26 pm, he sat at a table overhung by broad bright green leaves at the Chestnut Café until he was given a sandwich and asked to leave. An observation officer noted he picked a tulip – pink – and placed it in the fold of his book. He again returned to 'Le Tambour'.

On the third day, he walked north. He entered the 'Cinema Majestic Bastille' and started watching the first of what would be a continuous reel of *Nouvelle Vague* cinema black and white classics. It pays to point out that conducting surveillance on Ernst Stammers was difficult. Us older officers needed to sleep regular hours; the juniors who watched him nights, needed sleep during the days. Ernst Stammers never slept, he dozed. He nodded off while reading, his head in a holding pattern of slow forward neck leans broken by jerking head lifts as he realized he was sleeping. Then he'd write a little in his notebook, and again return to pattern. He'd get up, walk to the café or the snack bar, do nothing of significance, then again return to watch films and intermittently sleep. The only thing he actually bought was a monstrous cotton candy. A bag as long as his arm of fluffy pink cotton candy that caught the light from the cinema screen with every white pause.

I actually sat there watching the films and observing him for around six hours. The black and white cinema sucks you in so deep that your mind starts filling in the colors where there's none. Blacks become browns, purples and blues; grays become anything and everything; and whites become yellows, greens, and... pinks. That's when the absurd idea hit me.

Ernst Stammers had followed a path dominated by

colors. The first day was red. The second day was green, and the third was black, white and gray. Each day he'd attached himself to something pink. It only made sense in a corny, roundabout, *Hardy Boys*, *Nancy Drew*, or *Secret Seven* sort of way. Something I didn't dare mention to anyone until we returned to learn more about the first judge.

We returned with our reports on Ernst Stammers. He was a bum. The connection was a dead end. He did nothing of consequence, and the mystery of his existence rested in the pages of notebook in which he scribbled constantly, probably writing a novel that would neither be published nor read by anyone.

The fate of the first judge changed everything. His name was Archie 'Red' O'Hare. Dependent on who you asked, he was so named because of the bright red hair he sported as a youth or because of his affiliation with leftist causes. His latest novel suggests it was the latter. It was a comical and cynical tale about bumbling security services trying to infiltrate and disrupt the Australian Communist Party. He was a renowned Australian author who'd popularized characterizations of his home country despite not living there since leaving in his twenties. He was now 72.

Archie 'Red' O'Hare was hit by an express train exiting a tunnel. There were no witnesses. It may have been suicide, nobody ever really knows what's going on inside a writer's head; it may have been an accident, he had a considerable amount of alcohol in his system, many writers do; or, it could have been murder.

The death of Red O'Hare took the case to another level. The Police Minister received calls from journalists, the Australian Embassy, and the contacts of every Penn Fiction Prize judge. She called the Commissioner, who called the Superintendent – probably about golf, but also to put pressure on him to get the case out of the way. Ten further officers were assigned to the case. Their first debriefing was on the story itself by our most informed reader, college boy DC Cleaver.

'It's a 2,989-word piece entitled *Burgerflippers*. It fits all the eligibility requirements for the Penn Fiction Prize competition. On the surface, it appears to fit the detective fiction genre…'

'So do you, college boy!' Cleaver's upper-class accent, and his education, made him an easy target. And a particularly easy target for a working-class Glaswegian like Jimmy Doogan. But Cleaver gave as good as he got. 'Listen,' he started, 'if you could bloody well read more than the Beano over your bloody porridge, I wouldn't have to do this.'

The Chief Inspector entered, and Cleaver continued.

'The story appears to fit the detective fiction genre… but is actually a play on it to lull the reader into expecting a certain outcome. On the surface, the story is about a detective who investigates an author thought to be killing judges in a literary prize in order to scare the judges into awarding him the prize…'

'But that's what's happening here, is it not?'

DC Cleaver replied with an over-confident upper-class, 'Yes. Thanks, Doogan.' He then continued. 'There are five judges in the literary prize…' Doogan's body leaned forward. If he had a tail, it would've been wagging uncontrollably.

Cleaver paused and looked at him. 'What Doogan?'

'I'm sorry, but is this in the story or in real life? Now there's only four judges alive in real life, but are there five alive in the story? What does that mean?'

DC Cleaver looked at the Chief Inspector in frustration and shrugged his shoulders. The Chief Inspector took the floor.

'Listen, the story appears to be a threat. With the death of Red O'Hare, it now appears that whoever wrote it, has taken steps to fulfil that threat.' He stepped back, 'Continue Cleaver.'

'The first judge to die in the story was Mr Red, so named because of his alcohol-stained ruddiness. It also happens to match Red O'Hare.'

'And the Super!' someone spat out from the back. Cleaver continued.

'The next to die in the story was Ms Green, then Mr Black, Ms White, Ms Gray, and last of all Ms Pink – they appear to match figures in our investigation. Ms Green could relate to the second judge's green streak through her hair. Mr Black, well, you're aware the third judge is black, and Ms White, well, she's white...'

'Oh c'mon, this is going too far. Are we really...?' The Chief Inspector put an immediate stop to Kassim's outcry. Cleaver again continued.

'And as you're aware, the fifth judge is Pinkie Ong – the Parisian socialite and author of several recently successful texts.'

It was at that point at which I drew a connection to Ernst Stammers' color-dominated path around Paris. We'd followed Ernst Stammers and seen him take whole days dominated by red, green, black, white and gray. I informed Cleaver and the Chief Inspector. Bunson and I were to be sent back to Paris to break through the third wall – we were to talk to Ernst Stammers and, if we decided so, pull him in for questioning.

In the process of arranging our return visit, we learned he'd already been collared. The French took him in for breaking his restraining order. He was arrested banging on the doors of the concierge at the building which housed Pinkie Ong's apartment. He spent a day in lock-up, was sent for state assessment, and released to the American Hospital of Paris for psychiatric treatment. We received scanned copies of his checked-in materials – namely the notebook. It was a penned copy of the story with lines scratched out and additions put in place. He was rewriting it. He discharged himself after one day and disappeared.

The Chief Inspector, Superintendent, DCs Cleaver, Bunson, Doogan, and I entered the consultation room. I introduced everyone. The judges looked nervous. DC Cleaver gave them all the information we had – save the less than conclusive color connection. The Chief Inspector gave them our proposal.

'We want to notify Ernst Stammers that he's won the Penn Fiction Prize.' He explained what would be required and why. The idea was to draw him out, collar him, and then investigate. The judges looked at each other and then Pinkie Ong spoke up.

'Well, we've been thinking. It's actually a really good story. And to be frank, the story was going to be awarded to Red O'Hare's toy boy lover to get him to sign over his next novel.' She looked at the publisher, who immediately stepped forward.

'Really, this happens in short story competitions all the time. It's not anything unusual – if there's good writing, we still reach out to authors, but just not with the first prize.' Her voice lowered in tone with the last words. The third judge stepped forward; his much deeper voice contrasted sharply.

'Look, we don't think we need to offer him the prize in ruse. We all agree, he's the winner.'

The Chief Inspector shook his head in confusion. 'The man was assessed as a paranoid schizophrenic by French authorities – he may well be dangerous.' He turned to Pinkie Ong. 'He was caught banging on the door of your apartment building.'

'Inspector, do you know how many people bang on that door every night? It's a short walk from Paris's oldest Scottish pub and next to a brothel...'

At that point Doogan couldn't help himself and let out a clichéd remark. 'Ah, the Auld Alliance? I know that place, it's brilliant!'

Twenty days later, at a ceremony in Paris, Ernst Stammers was awarded the Penn Paris Fiction Prize. On the same day, I received the notebook he abandoned when he suddenly left the American Hospital of Paris. I looked over the corrections of the story. In the borders of the text on the second to last page was one line that stayed with me. 'You only have to kill one judge to win a short story competition.'

Silo

By Richard Hooton

Born and brought up in Mansfield, Nottinghamshire, Richard Hooton studied English Literature at the University of Wolverhampton before becoming a journalist and communications officer. He has had numerous short stories published and has been listed in various competitions, including winning contests run by Segora, Artificium Magazine, Henshaw Press, Evesham Festival of Words, Cranked Anvil, the Charroux Prize for Short Fiction, the Federation of Writers (Scotland) Vernal Equinox Competition and the Hammond House International Literary Prize. Richard lives in Mossley, near Manchester.

'Silo wants you dead.'

Petr's words echo around the Old Bailey courtroom.

'That's what I heard. Peering down Wapping Old Stairs, its algae coat glinting in the moonlight, I saw two figures standing on the river's blackened fringe, silhouetted against the night sky. One fell to his knees, head bowed. The other looming over him, arm outstretched, gun in his hand. Everything froze. It was like... it was like being trapped in a nightmarish painting, only my heart able to move. The Thames lapping against the rocks. The briny stench of seawater. The gun...'

Petr looks each of the jury in the eye. He's described that scene to the police, the CPS. Now them. Every detail matches.

The thin, bespectacled prosecutor nods. 'What happened next?'

Sitting alone, dark suit taut on his lean, muscular figure, Petr grips the smooth witness stand, not a single split blemishing its solid oak surface. A deep breath. 'The gun had a long, slim end. A silencer or something. Just made this stifled crack. The man on his knees crumpled, sprawled across driftwood.'

'Then what?'

'I turned and fled. Back down the alleyway, onto Wapping High Street. Couldn't stop until I was safe.'

'The gunman didn't follow you?'

Petr rubs his bald scalp. 'Don't know. Never looked back. Just ran. Only stopped when I reached others. Then called the police.'

The prosecutor turns to the jury. 'Following my witness's emergency call, several Metropolitan Police officers were despatched to the location where the victim, a Mr Mikhail Morozov, was discovered deceased from a single gunshot wound to the forehead.'

He turns back to Petr. 'Did you see the gunman's face?'

Petr swallows. 'Yes. After firing, he turned.'

The prosecutor holds up his palm. Returns to the jury. 'My witness identified the gunman, using video identification, as Ivan Kalashnik. The gun used in the murder was found during a trawl of the river. Mr Kalashnik has since vanished. He is an associate of the defendant Oleksiy Silchenko, also known as Silo.'

Petr feels Silo's glare burn through the red curtain that separates them like acid consuming skin. He just stares straight at the jury.

The prosecutor studies his notes over wire-framed glasses. 'This murder has its roots in the former Soviet Union. A tug-of-war over Crimea between Russia and Ukraine, and over Ukraine between Russia and Europe. This blood-soaked power battle is now being played out on London's streets.'

Twelve blank faces.

He explains how Crimea was controversially annexed by Russia in 2014. How Ukraine considers the Black Sea peninsula to be under hostile Russian occupation, but Russia claims to have liberated a strategically important region rightfully and historically theirs. How repercussions resulted in thousands of Ukrainians killed in skirmishes, while Western sanctions have pushed the Russian economy to the brink of recession.

Petr studies the oak-panelled courtroom. Breathes in its history. The prosecutor continues; a professor lecturing children. 'Mr Silchenko is a former colonel of the Ukrainian Ground Force's Operation Command South. After Crimea was lost, he sought sanctuary in London.'

The jury shuffle on their pews.

'The victim is a former army general of the Russian Federation's Ground Forces who fought in Crimea. He fell out of favour with the Russian government after being accused of spying for America. Exiled in London, it appears his path crossed with Mr Silchenko. Mr Morozov was executed in revenge for his role in Crimea. While Mr Silchenko did not pull the trigger, it is the Crown's case that he ordered this assassination, a crime he perhaps would have got away with were it not for my witness.'

He turns to the judge seated on high, whose violet gown swamps his slight frame, his rigid wig lopsided. 'No further questions, Your Honour.'

The defence barrister springs to his feet, lips curling as if tasting something unpleasant. 'Remind us, where were you going when you just happened to pass at that exact moment?'

Petr takes a sip of water. 'Home. I'd passed a churchyard when I heard voices from the alleyway, sounding as if... someone was pleading.'

The barrister tilts his head, eyes narrowing. 'And you followed? Down a dark alleyway? In the dead of night?'

Petr balances the glass on the edge of the witness stand. 'Cautiously. To see what was happening. The alleyway opens into a dockyard where the steps are.'

'And you're certain of what you heard?'

'I heard him clearly.'

'"Silo wants you dead."'

'Exactly.'

'You're certain of the word "Silo"? He couldn't have said something else? Milo? Sila? Filo? Some other word?'

Petr focuses on the jury. 'Without doubt.'

'And despite the darkness and the situation, you got a clear view of the gunman's face?'

'As clear to me as yours is now.'

The barrister retreats to his bench with a weary sigh. 'No further questions, Your Honour.'

The judge faces Petr. 'I'd like to thank you for your bravery in giving evidence in such circumstances. You're free to leave.'

An usher waddles to Petr's side. Beckons. He follows her through a side door, along a corridor and into a small room. She gestures for him to sit in a plastic chair. 'Must feel good to get the truth out, love?'

Petr leans against the wall.

She tilts her head. 'Here on your own?'

He says nothing.

The usher shrugs. 'Suit yourself. Just wait there. Witness protection will be here in a mo.'

She closes the door behind her.

Petr counts to ten. Eases the door open. Checks the corridor. Empty. He follows the route taken when escorted out for a cigarette break. Reaches the Grand Hall. Stops to gaze at the neo-baroque style ceiling and walls, white marble flecked with black swirls. The towering dome, bronze busts and gilded paintings remind him of St Petersburg. He drinks in the axioms decorating the walls:

'Right lives by law and law subsists by power.'

'Poise the cause in justice's equal scales.'

Petr steps outside. Looks up at Lady Justice on the dome, sword in her right hand, scales of justice in her left. The inscription: 'DEFEND THE CHILDREN OF THE POOR & PUNISH THE WRONGDOER'.

He smiles coolly. Heads down Newgate Street, merging into the city centre crowd like vodka in water. Reaches Millennium Bridge. A lone figure in a long black coat, arms resting on the guard rail, looks out across the rushing waters of the Thames, tourists bustling by.

Petr joins his side. 'It is done. They'll sum up then send the jury out. Could reach verdict tomorrow.'

The bearded man nods, a Belomor cigarette gripped

between his lips. Ash tumbles past the collar of his shearling-lined leather coat. He takes out a paper wallet from an inside pocket and passes it to Petr, his eyes never leaving the river. 'Your ticket. Your flight leaves tonight.'

Studying The Shard, a jagged knifepoint piercing the clouds, Petr sniffs. 'I'll be glad to leave this ugly country. All these glass towers and that giant hamster wheel spinning by the river.'

The man draws hard on his cigarette. Smoke billows. 'I have grown to like it. The smaller your view becomes, the more you appreciate another's landscape. My wife and children would be happy here.' His eyes slick marbles. 'And I would do anything to protect them.'

A strong gust sways the bridge. The man takes a final drag, blows a coil of smoke, then flicks the cigarette butt to the floor. Crushes it with a stamp and twist of his boot. '*Udachi*, Comrade.'

Petr spits into the river. 'To the devil, Alexey Volkov.'

Alexey disappears into the shadows.

Thoughts occupied by his passport and bag, Petr heads in the opposite direction. Turns right at St Paul's Cathedral. Passes a red telephone box, Victorian lamp-posts and a red double-decker bus. Like stepping back in time. A tide of people flow past. He analyses each one. Not far from the Underground now. Petr's head stiffens, nose twitching. A glimpse behind. Two black-clad men in his slipstream, stern expressions looking right through him. Petr stops in front of a clothes store. Admires a pin-striped suit in the window. Watches their reflections. Their subtle glances.

Petr counts to five. Then walks with a purpose. Swerves into a shopping centre. Looks back.

They're following.

He curves around a group. Shoves others out the way. Leaves the centre and indignant shouts. Glimpses. A gust opens one of the men's coats revealing a gun tucked into his belt. Petr swerves down a deserted side street, the station a few hundred yards away.

A white transit van, windows tinted, tears around the corner. Speeds towards him. Petr swivels. The men just behind, satisfied smirks. The van screeches to a halt.

Hands grab Petr. Lock his arms. Someone shoves a sack over his head. Everything black.

'Stay quiet.'

A door slides open. They push him inside. Heat and diesel fumes replace cold, crisp air. The door slams shut. Meaty hands press him against the floor.

'Stay still.'

A deep, guttural voice. Ukrainian accent. 'Silo wants you alive.'

Petr controls his breathing. 'Where you taking me?'

'No talking.'

Petr counts the hands holding him. Four men. Listens intently. Gears crunch. The van jolts as it turns. Grumbles forward. Accelerates. He imagines a map of London. Cheapside. A40. Past St Paul's. The Old Bailey. Everything's still: traffic lights. Engines rev. Horns blare. The van lurches forward.

After several turns, the map fades.

The van finally halts. Petr remains ragdoll limp as he's dragged into cool air then bundled inside a building. They haul him upstairs, each step whacking against his feet. Shunt him into a room, then on a stool. Footsteps all around. The sack torn away in a burst of stinging light.

Small room. Stained mattress in one corner. Unvarnished floorboards. Peeling white paint. No window. One door. A bare bulb hangs from the ceiling.

Petr's eyes settle on a large man sitting in a chair. Hawkish eyebrows. Flattened nose. Mole on chin.

'What is your name?' A shards-of-ice voice. The same south Ukrainian accent.

'My name is Peter Smith.' Petr allows his voice to tremble. The man sniffs. 'Your real name?'

'Peter Smith. I swear.'

The man shakes his head. Two men built like Caucasian Ovcharka dogs enter the room, shut the door, stand either side of him.

The man takes a walnut and a silver steel nutcracker from his pocket. 'Your occupation?'

'I'm just a businessman. I sell fitness equipment.'

'That is what it says on your profile pages.' He places the walnut in the vice. Squeezes. 'But it is not true.'

A crack. The walnut splits, shell crumbling to the floor. 'Nothing corroborates this.'

'You've got it wrong.' Petr lets his face crumple, incredulity spiking his tone.

The trio eyes him.

'Why have you framed Silchenko?' The man holds the two halves of wrinkled nut, like shrunken brains, in his palm. 'Who pays you to lie?'

'I am Peter Smith. A 35-year-old divorced dad from Brixton. Please, I have two children. I'm not lying. Nobody's paid me.'

The man laughs. 'Your English accent is good but not faultless.'

Petr stretches curling fingers. Counts soundlessly to ten. 'Please. You've made a mistake.'

'Whatever, Peter Smith... such a plain name.'

He tosses the nut into his mouth. Crunches. 'Here's what will happen. Tomorrow we return you to court where you will tell the judge the truth.'

Petr analyses him. The coldness in his eyes. The steady pulse in the artery of his neck. The relaxed breathing.

'Which is?'

'We both know you never saw or heard what you claimed. Withdraw your testimony and the case will be thrown out.'

'Then what?'

'You'll be free.' The man chews. 'Try to alert anyone and we hunt you down. Kill you and your family.'

Petr lowers his head.

'Sleep here.'

The man drags his chair out, its legs scraping the floor. The others follow. A key clinks in the lock.

Petr slumps onto the mattress. Stares at the ceiling, scenarios battling in his mind.

Time crawls.

Until a key turns again. The door opens. Sack. Dragged. Van. A repeated journey.

It stops. The sack's torn away.

'You know what you must do.'

Petr squints at the Old Bailey's weathered stone. Staggers inside. 'I need to speak to the judge in the Silchenko case.'

The security guard examines him.

'I'm the witness.'

The guard beckons Petr through the scanner then signals to a colleague, whispering something in his ear.

'Wait here.' The guard scuttles down a corridor.

Petr watches the colleague deal with people passing through the scanner. At the opportune moment, he slips inside. He pictures every option. All exits covered. Only one way out.

Petr finds the door. Loiters until it creaks ajar. A woman passes through, mop and bucket clanging. Before the door swing shuts, Petr slides through the gap.

He follows the route of the historical tour two months previously: through the abandoned Newgate Prison underneath the courtrooms, and along Dead Man's Walk where prisoners once marched to the gallows. White-tiled walls yellowed. A pervading smell of mildew. Archways progressively narrower until squeezing through; a matryoshka doll system. A circular staircase. Petr releases the dense air he's been holding. Then clambers down into the building's bowels.

The old coal cellar. An eerie silence punctuated by dripping water and rumbling trains. Petr heaves a metal grill from the floor. Peers into the black mouth, the River Fleet roaring past below.

A deep breath. Petr scrambles down the ladder. Leaps. Water splashes his legs, writhes around his ankles. The open hatch a moon. He wades until the weak light fades, then feels his way along the slimy brick wall. The culverted river, hidden beneath London's masses, is no sewer but smells the same.

Petr ploughs on, feet numb, icy tentacles reaching up his calves. Light pierces the gloom, exposing a ladder's outline. He hauls himself up, reaching an iron grid, the light splitting through its gaps. Leaning against the ladder, Petr shoves and shoves. The grid yields, lifting up and away.

Petr pokes his head into daylight. Brakes squeal, wind whistling around him. A car grille halts a metre from his face. He wriggles out of the hole. Standing in the road, hands on the bonnet, he gulps air. Stares at the open-mouthed driver. Then looks around. The middle of a junction, a pub on the right, another further along. Street signs: Saffron Hill and Greville Road.

Passers-by gawk as Petr squelches along the street. 'Metropolitan Railway', adorns the top of a distinguished building, 'Farringdon Station' below. The map back in his mind. His apartment several stops away.

Petr freezes.

A distinctive white van, windows tinted.

He ducks into the packed station and descends into another underworld, this one with an inferno's heat. Reminds him of the recruitment video: the crackle and screaming as the defector was fed into the furnace, the crematorium chimney the only way out of the agency, the other recruits' faces green.

A waiting train. Petr pushes aboard. Settles into a corner, puddles forming at his sodden shoes, a stink to high heaven. Petr glares at a teenager whose headphones leak drum and bass. The carriage shudders into movement. The train jolts forwards and backwards.

Petr's trousers and shoes are dry when he reaches his apartment. It's as he left it, every inch already scrubbed clean of any trace. Reaches for his bag on the couch.

Four short raps on the door. Four heavier thuds. Two quick taps.

Petr checks the spyhole. Opens the door. '*Dobriy den*, Alexey Volkov.'

'Petr Kuznetsov.'

Alexey brushes past, the door clattering shut. 'You did not make your flight.' Alexey stands between Petr and the couch. 'And you look and smell like shit.'

Petr tells him everything.

Alexey's granite features don't flicker. 'The jury gave verdict. Guilty.'

Petr raises a fist. 'It worked. The traitor Morozov is dead and our enemy Silchenko behind bars. Two birds, one bullet. Don't betray or forsake us.'

Alexey remains as still as the room. Dusk's gradual darkness descending.

'It was better in the past, Alexey. With men like Silo on our side, the Soviet Union was more powerful. When the Ukraine rejoins the motherland, things will be how they were.'

Alexey looks away. 'Those days will not return.'

Petr frowns. 'Once Kiev overthrows the Western coup, we will rule as one.'

'The Soviet Union is long gone.'

Petr jabs a finger. 'Crimea is ours again, our naval base secure. With these Ukrainian traitors gone, Kiev will shake off its Western fleas, then return to its master.'

Alexey shakes his head. 'We can no longer behave as if stuck in the past. Such policies cause sanctions. Our people suffer. We must communicate and work with others, not isolated.'

Petr glares. 'I have never heard you speak this way.'

Alexey stares at the bag. 'Since military school, you have only ever known the GRU, Petr.'

'I never served as a paratrooper or with the Spetsnaz like you.'

'Your skills are better suited to elimination.' Alexey strokes his beard. 'Never knew your parents or family, did you?'

'The GRU is all I need.'

Alexey places his hand on the bag. 'What is it... three years working together?'

'I have never failed you.'

Petr steps forward to seize the bag. Alexey holds it down.

'Was life not better in the old days, Alexey?'

'Our country is crumbling. Those that can, that find the motivation, leave.'

'No one defects...'

Petr snatches the bag's handle. Alexey's weight anchors it. Petr tugs. Alexey sighs. Lets go.

Petr hauls the bag onto his shoulder. Moves towards the door. '*Bud zdorov*, Alexey.'

'*Proschai*, Petr.'

Something in his voice makes Petr turn around. He stares down the black hole of a silencer.

Alexey looks him in the eye.

'Silo wants you dead.'

The Door

By Belinda Stuebinger

Belinda recently graduated from the MA Creative Writing and Publishing at Bournemouth University and afterwards started her PhD, also in Bournemouth, researching fictional serial killers, making her hobby a profession. When she doesn't have her head in a book or her fingers flying across a keyboard, it is very likely you'll find a game console controller in her hand.

You never did tell me what was behind that door. Now that I know, I have to say I am disappointed. Not in what was behind that door – that actually surprised me – but I am disappointed in you. The relationship I thought we had was clearly not the same for you. And now, I am left here with the rest of my life and the knowledge that I was not enough.

That day, when I asked you about the door, you told me it was just some storage cupboard. And I believed you. How stupid and gullible was I? It was a rainy day that day. I walked through half of town to get to you.

I remember when I turned up at your doorstep you were surprised. 'Veronica, I didn't think you'd make it in this rain!'

'I'll always make it to you,' I said with a cheeky smile on my face, 'even if I have to walk because I'm too poor to afford a bus ticket.'

'Don't talk about yourself like that. Times will be better soon when you can earn your own money.'

And then you pulled me closer. That was what I came for after all. At least, that's how it all started. I could feel you, pressed firmly against me. It reminded me of the first time. I was so afraid, but I went with it. I wanted it, despite how afraid I was. My lips now met yours. Your stubble was almost unbearable, but I ignored it. More important things were going on, and you never liked it when I talked while we were doing our thing. Your mouth wandered to my neck and my glance wandered to the door. It was so white. It looked almost sterile. My thoughts must have wandered a little too far away.

'What is it?' you asked.

'You never told me what is behind this door,' I said, pulling away from you and slowly walking towards the door.

You lunged in front of me. Not that I could have opened

it. There was no handle. Just a keyhole.

'There is nothing important behind this, just a storage cupboard,' you said.

I should have known better then. I should have seen the lie glistening in your eyes. Why didn't I, you ask? Simple. I wanted you. And I didn't want anything standing in the way of it.

So I said, 'OK.'

And pulled you back towards me. Pressed myself against you this time. Ignoring the painful stubble, I kissed you. And there it was. You kissed me back. Feeling your tongue on mine. It was like a drug. And I was addicted. You picked me up and carried me upstairs. I had always admired your house. It was so big. Enough room for a whole family. But there was only you. And now me. I know I liked the excitement. Being with you made me feel alive. Did it have the opposite effect for you?

I always wondered who decorated your bedroom. It clearly had a woman's touch, but, back then, I didn't think about it too much. I know you weren't married at the time because we were together too often. There was no way you could have hidden a wife from me. But you did hide things from me, didn't you? Your bed was soft, one of those that you sink in when you let yourself fall into it. I took off your shirt and started on your jeans. My dress was already unzipped on the way up, so I just slipped out of it. I could feel your hands caress my body. Touching me. Everywhere. I know you don't like it if I say 'no', so I don't. I let you lead. It is like dancing tango. The most erotic dance there is. It is the man who leads, not the woman. It doesn't matter if I truly enjoyed it. You did. I wanted you to be happy. I wanted to do everything to make sure you were mine. So, I only made the noises you wanted me to make. Until you finished. It didn't matter if I had finished. All that mattered was to give you the relief that you so desperately needed. Now I know how that sounds, but I was addicted. I was addicted to your pleasure.

Maybe wanting to keep you was selfish. Maybe it was wrong. But it's how I felt. How I still feel if I'm very honest. And that's what I'm here to do, after all.

Afterwards, you lit a cigarette, as always. We laid in your bed, both smoking from this one cigarette. And for a moment, the world would stand still. Then you took your picture, and it was done for the day. You always took these pictures. I thought I was special to you. I thought you loved me. When I left, you stuck your hand up my skirt and kissed me.

Then pushed me outside and said, 'We'll meet again, young lady.'

That was the last time I saw you. The last time I felt you. They say pride comes before a fall; well, the fall was hard. A few days after, someone knocked on our door. My mother opened and I was called into the kitchen. She sat there, with the town's police officer. A bunch of pictures were in a box in front of her. Your pictures. But there weren't just pictures of me. The officer told us there were at least 15 other girls in here, if not more. He couldn't go through them all. First, my mother slapped me after the officer left. Then, she hugged me. It felt like forever. I didn't know what was going on. All I knew was that the officer said you were no longer with us. They found you in the room behind the door, hanging from the ceiling. My mother locked me in the flat when she left for work. I was alone. You were gone. You had left me. Not just that. That special relationship I thought we had? You had this with other girls too. You took the same pictures of other girls. I had overheard the officer tell my mother that your wife left you because you touched your own daughter when she was my age. I knew that was wrong. But what was so wrong about us? I needed you. I needed to make you happy. Even if I clearly couldn't give you enough happiness to stay.

'I have arranged for you to go and see someone,' my mother told me at the breakfast table the next morning.

'See who?' I asked her.

'Someone who can help you.'

I still didn't know why I needed help. It took me years to understand what happened between you and me. What you did to me. What you broke inside of me, without me even knowing that it was broken. And now, I'm messed up. I don't know, I will never know, if what I'm feeling is true or forced. All my life, since I can remember, I wanted to be with you. I still do. They tell me it is wrong how I feel, but I can't help it. And God is my witness, I have tried, but I love you. I need you. I need to be with you. So now, I'm in my own locked room. And soon, I will be with you again.

Judgement

By Richard Hooton

Born and brought up in Mansfield, Nottinghamshire, Richard Hooton studied English Literature at the University of Wolverhampton before becoming a journalist and communications officer. He has had numerous short stories published and has been listed in various competitions, including winning contests run by Segora, Artificium Magazine, Henshaw Press, Evesham Festival of Words, Cranked Anvil, the Charroux Prize for Short Fiction, the Federation of Writers (Scotland) Vernal Equinox Competition and the Hammond House International Literary Prize. Richard lives in Mossley, near Manchester.

This ancient courtroom has undoubtedly heard many voices over the decades, echoing between the oak-panelled walls. Mr Cole's was nothing unusual, his flat, northern vowels recounting a tale as old as time immemorial, a sad situation, often repeated. Something about the case troubles me though.

A wooden door creaks open to allow the jury to file back in. I scrutinise Mr Cole in the glass-encased dock. A man small in stature, his hair grey and receding, his face a roadmap of lines. *Guilty or innocent?* In the next few minutes, he'll either be serving life or free. For it's the most heinous of crimes: murder. A huge responsibility for those making the decision. Lives hang in the balance for others to decide on like Greek gods playing with mortals.

I reposition the red sash across my violet gown and adjust my rigid, grey wig. Must look presentable. These noble traditions are important. At home I'm Ron to my better half, Ronald to the guests. Here, I am Mr Justice Goldsmith. People stand when I enter the courtroom. Listen intently to my every word. Bow to me, before they leave.

Usually, I'm certain as to the defendant's guilt or otherwise. But this case has left me most confounded, causing me to relay proceedings over and over in my mind. Fortunately, I have an excellent memory. I don't need my papers to recall the evidence.

The particulars are these: John and Linda Cole met thirty-two years ago and were married within two years. Mr Cole is a 55-year-old science lecturer at the local university, a former polytechnic. His wife, three years his junior, is a humble housewife who gave up her own blossoming career in law to stay at home and look after the children, as per tradition. Their son and daughter have long grown up and flew the nest as soon as possible. There seems nothing remarkable about this middle-class couple. However, Mrs Cole has simply vanished into thin air having not been seen for 18 months. The prosecution state that she is dead — and that her husband killed her.

Where's the evidence?

Aye, there's the rub. The prosecution's case is weak. I do not rate this prosecutor, Davina Barren QC. Far too wet behind the ears, all kohl-rimmed eyes and sulky pout. I doubt she's taken on a case of this magnitude before. She's too quiet, stumbles frequently and has even overstepped the mark on occasion. I have lost my patience with her quite a few times, ordering her to find the right files or get to the point. More mouse than matador; she never grasped the bull by the horns.

Admittedly, she did have a tremendous hurdle to overcome: the body has never been found. Without it, there is no forensic evidence of the ultimate misdeed. A jury is always nervous to convict without modern science to back them. And, obviously, there was no testimony from the supposed victim.

I watch the jurors carefully as one by one they enter the courtroom. They certainly represent all aspects of society: an acne-marked student with little life experience to guide him (I had to bark at him on the first day to remove his chewing gum); a mature lady, part of the twinset and pearls brigade; a confident businessman who asserted his control by taking the role of foreman. I could go on. But I have little time left to get a peg on this case before they inform me of their decision. I must think hard about the evidence. There were, in fact, some forensics.

'Blood spattering. On the kitchen wall,' Ms Barren had informed the jury. 'DNA tests prove it's Mrs Cole's blood. The crown's case is that it's from a fatal injury sustained after a violent row with this defendant.' She hesitated, losing her train of thought, and I glared at her. 'W-w-while cleaning up, Mr Cole, he missed this spot.' She got back on track, thankfully. 'More traces of blood were found. In Mr Cole's car, er, in the boot. We ascertain this was from when he disposed of the body.'

David Wright QC, defending, had given a contemptuous sigh. An excellent barrister, always gives a faultless performance, and a fine fellow — I've enjoyed many a bottle of Château Haut-Brion with him at a gala dinner. He's extremely witty. And can destroy a supposition in a flash.

Mr Wright easily explained it away as Mrs Cole having previously cut herself while preparing vegetables, cleaning up the finger wound and the mess, but then later aggravating the injury and bleeding again while transporting her shopping from the boot. 'Such a tiny speck of blood is no indication of murder,' he surmised.

That's the essence of a trial. The prosecutor constructs his case like any good builder: a solid base from the agreed facts, carefully cementing each brick of evidence in place with a thick layer of emphasis, the edifice strong and unshakeable. The defence swings his words like a wrecking ball, hoping to demolish it. This Barren woman, her case is a house of cards.

It's a shame as I adore the cut and thrust when two fine adversaries clash in the coliseum of the courtroom, their rapier-sharp jabs aiming to hack each other's case to shreds. I fear Ms Barren is just not in Mr Wright's league. Must be 25 years since I was called to the bar. How I loved to test my intellect against the finest minds of my generation, to spot the flaws in their argument and devise a strategy to expose them. But a higher purpose was calling. I wanted to be a judge, so I took my first steps as a recorder and after tests and interviews I succeeded. Now I sit above the fray: observing, ruling, oiling the wheels of our fine criminal justice system. Focusing on the facts to remain impartial, objective, unprejudiced. These barristers are knights in my realm, the rest pawns being moved around the chessboard. I digress. What happened next?

'How did he dispose of the body?' Ms Barren posed. 'Well, he could have easily buried poor Mrs Cole somewhere only he knows, or an incinerator would do the job. Not too tricky a task for a man with his scientific knowledge.'

'There is nothing to confirm that Linda Cole is dead,' growled Mr Wright, pacing the courtroom. 'On the contrary, text messages show she was enjoying a new life.'

Yes, the text messages. Sent to relatives — after the date on which Mrs Cole was supposedly killed.

'I've left John. Please don't be upset. You know we've drifted apart,' read one.

'I've gone away to gather my thoughts. There's no one else involved.'

'Don't be worried. I'm OK. Just need some time to myself.'

All written in the same calm prose.

'No one's spoken to or seen Linda Cole in the last 18 months,' said Ms Barren. 'Could it be that she didn't send these messages? That they are, in fact, a smokescreen? Mobile phone records show they were all sent from within a 20-mile radius. If Mrs Cole has run away, then she's not bothered to go far. And without anyone bumping into her in 18 months.'

Mrs Cole's reluctance to meet or talk about her sudden flight is what led to relatives and friends reporting her as a missing person. These text messages have since dried up.

That's where the defence's key witnesses came in. Two experts who analysed Mrs Cole's messages before and after her alleged demise could see no difference in their style, the language used or the mannerisms. They appear to be from her.

You do get what you pay for when using expert witnesses.

'Is she sending these messages from beyond the grave,' smirked Mr Wright.

Unfortunately, Mr Cole's mobile was of no help, having been accidentally dropped into a washing-up bowl and damaged beyond repair.

All twelve of the jury are in the room now. I feel drained. People don't realise how much of an intellectually and emotionally demanding role this is. They think we just sit here dozing off and spouting drivel. Luckily, I never stop thinking. I must concentrate on what was said. Time is of the essence.

We were plunged into the dark pool of domestic abuse. Mrs Cole had made a few calls to the police over the years about physical and mental harm but had never pressed charges so there's nothing of substance there. In fact, she actually has a conviction herself for assaulting her husband, a Section 20 wounding without intent for slicing his arm with a knife. She pleaded guilty, in mitigation claiming self-defence after being provoked. Regardless of the truth, the conviction is there on her criminal record. She was sentenced to community service.

Family and friends spoke of a troubled marriage. Ms Barren encouraged them in their descriptions of Mrs Cole as a timid, browbeaten woman, left subservient to her domineering husband. Mr Wright correctly dismissed it as tittle-tattle and I struck most of these testimonies out as irrelevant, overruling Ms Barren's objections and ignoring the arched eyebrow she raised.

Mr Cole's character references were much more pertinent. His university colleagues and management described him as a dedicated, upstanding individual, faultless in his work and single-minded in his attention to detail. Students' claims of a temper were batted back: 'just a means of controlling a class.'

The prosecution pointed out that the perpetrator is often someone close to you. Their star witness was the next-door neighbour Maureen Davies, which takes us back to their prediction of when Mrs Cole died, for she heard arguments erupting from the semi-detached house. These had been increasing until one almighty row after which Mrs Cole hasn't been seen since.

The frail spinster described it as 'an awful racket. Had to turn my telly right up.'

Mr Wright eyed his quarry with a hungry look. He moved swiftly as he spoke. 'Did you actually hear anything said between them?'

'Heard enough effing and blinding to know it were nasty.'

'But no specific words, Miss Davies.'

'No... but it were a fight.'

'Now, now, Miss Davies. It was just a row, wasn't it?'

She paused, nose scrunched, lips pursed. 'I heard things smashing.'

'A dropped glass. Nothing sinister. Do you watch a lot of TV, Miss Davies? Might your imagination have got the better of you?'

The look of a startled rabbit in his headlights. Sworn to tell the truth. Scared of getting it wrong. She looked up at me. I couldn't help her. You have to allow the knight some leeway to be forthright and get to the truth.

'I, erm, I thought... it sounded nasty.'

Mr Wright pounced. 'You thought. But you heard no specific threats, no specific noises.'

'I can't be sure what I...'

'No. You can't be sure. You had your TV on loud,

focusing on what you were viewing weren't you, dear.'

Mr Wright ended with a flourish, his black gown cascading through the air behind him. The prey was down. She stumbled from the witness stand in a daze, Mr Wright casting a sympathetic smile.

The jury is almost at their seats. I am running out of time. What else was there? The crux of a case is often exposed in the defendant's testimony. That is where I must focus.

I had studied the accused intently as he made his way to the stand. Hunched and gaunt, Mr Cole moved slowly. He gripped the edge of the stand's wooden frame to keep himself upright. His dark suit hung baggy on his slight frame, his shirt a touch creased, the plain tie loose on the collar. For all the world a man in need of a woman's touch.

Ms Barren was running out of chances to land a blow. 'Talk me through the events of that night,' she demanded.

My courtroom is a quiet place. I insist on it. Even so, there was an eerie hush as everyone strained to hear his testimony. Mr Cole spoke falteringly, as if every word was painful.

'As Lin said in her texts, we'd drifted apart.' His voice struggled to carry across the dry air. It held no echo, barely reaching the panelled walls never mind rebounding. 'Distant. We became distant. Just rows. No violence.'

I stared at him over the rim of my spectacles. No tell-tale giveaways: none of the nervous twitches or biting of the lip or looking away that I have observed of the guilty over the years. Like a curmudgeon, his face gave away nothing.

Ms Barren was scratching around. 'What did you say to her?'

'I said I don't want to be with you anymore. She was shocked that I'd said it. Then she walked out.'

'That was it? No argument?'

'No.'

'So your neighbours who heard shouting are lying?'

'Just mistaken.'

'Your wife walked out of thirty-two years of marriage without a whimper?'

'She left to start a new life,' Mr Cole said softly. He looked at the jury with the expression of a man bereft, a man left all alone. Then stared at the ground as he mumbled: 'I miss her.'

I examined the defendant. I saw no guilt, no malice, no evil in him.

I remember glancing up at the public gallery at that moment. Mrs Cole's elderly mother was sitting on her own, hands clasped as if in prayer, a fretful expression worn into her face, her eyes suddenly screwing tight shut. Sadly, she may never know what happened to her daughter.

Mr Wright's summing up was a masterclass.

'Where's the body?' he demanded of the jury. 'Where's the murder weapon? Where's the proof?' He slammed a fist into his palm at the end of each sentence. 'With no proof, the verdict is not guilty. No body... not guilty. No weapon... not guilty.' Mr Wright gave the jury a winsome smile. He'd planted doubt in their minds and stood back to let it grow.

I have to agree with him. There's nothing to show that Mr Cole has committed murder. I am quite certain now that he's innocent. The poor man has been put through the wringer after losing his wife. There must be some other explanation as to what's happened to her.

In my summing up, I talked the jury through the lack of evidence. 'You must be beyond reasonable doubt to convict,' I'd brusquely informed them. They sat in silence on their wooden pews like well-behaved children, gazing up at me on my bench. It is my job to guide them, to steer them through the muddied waters of conjecture and into the clearer flow of fact, while keeping them well away from the perilous waterfalls of modern temptations (don't discuss this case with your family and friends, I used to order juries; now I have to insist that they don't inform the world on social media, or google the defendant's past to help them make a decision.) I cleared their minds of the trivial and inconsequential, focusing their brainpower on the key issues at hand.

Now, as they take their seats, they are ready to give me their verdict. It's been three long days of deliberations. An uneasy feeling still stirs in me. As if, somehow, I've missed something of importance. But I've been over everything? It's so stifling in this windowless room, with no natural light, that it can be difficult to gather your thoughts. Like the guilty, the heat has nowhere to escape. There is also a fusty, damp odour, perhaps from years of decay, or maybe even from the evil that has festered between these walls, if that's not too fanciful.

The jury is all seated. The court reporter from the Evening News – a pretty little thing – has her pen poised. The clerk's fingers hover over her keyboard.

The endgame is upon us.

I scratch my head. Damn uncomfortable and itchy these wigs, especially in this temperature. Something else perturbs me. I remember now, there were other text messages, seemingly inconsequential. Ones sent by Mrs Cole to her friends.

'Don't worry about me. I'm in a good place.'

'I told him "I don't want to be with you anymore" and then I left.'

'I'm much happier now. Should have done this years ago.'

Wait. I've heard those words before in another context. The soft, gentle tone. 'I don't want to be with you anymore.'

It's his voice I hear, not hers. *His voice.* Mr Cole's made a mistake. Those experts have made a mistake. It was him. He wrote those text messages, not her.

I realise it's been silent in the courtroom for a few minutes. Everyone is waiting for me to speak. To finish this.

'Are you all right, Your Honour?' asks the clerk, turning round to glance at me. A trickle of sweat courses down my forehead.

I nod and look to the jury. Did they spot his crucial error?

'To the charge of murder, do you find the defendant guilty or not guilty?' My voice is shaky. There's nothing I can do.

The jury foreman stands. With a cough he clears his throat and speaks loudly and clearly, as I instructed him to.

'Not guilty,' echoes around this old, wooden cavern.

There's murmuring amongst the gallery, discontent, a shrill cry from the victim's mother followed by heaving sobs.

I hesitate as I lift my gavel. Then I bring it down with a dull thud.

'Not guilty,' I repeat with a croak, the words catching painfully in my throat.

I look Cole in the eye and the flicker of a sly smile creeps across his face. He stands taller, firmer, stronger.

'You are free to leave this courtroom,' I tell him hesitantly. 'An innocent man.'

Accurate to One-Sixteenth of an Ounce

By Jupiter Jones

Jupiter Jones lives in Wales and writes short and flash fictions. She is the winner of the Colm Tóibín International Prize and her stories have been published by Aesthetica, Brittle Star, Fish, Reflex Press. Her novella-in-flash, 'The Death and Life of Mrs Parker', is published by Ad Hoc Fiction.

Have you ever sat with a person while they died? It is
one of the most intimate moments imaginable. If they
are ready, and they go quietly, then it is respectful, more
respectful than birth. I don't think anyone is ever ready
for that: for being squeezed out, head-first. But death,
now that can be a quiet slipping through. Of course, if
the person dies while they are suspended on an industrial
weighing scale, then the intimacy will suffer. But they all
signed papers to give their consent. Not the dogs though.
They signed nothing.

Until a few months ago, I worked as an assistant to Doc
MacDougall, and he is as mad and as bitter as you have
heard tell. Perhaps you have read his papers, published
in the *Journal of the American Society for Psychical
Research*? Science, he calls it, but it seems to me now to
be a crock of shit, and I have cause to sorely regret my part
in it. That whole sorry business with the dogs began with
his housekeeper's pug. Butterball, Butty for short; he was
fat, and black with stumpy legs, and a tail that curled over
his short fat back bringing to mind a bacon pig. When the
housekeeper first noticed him missing from his basket in
the kitchen, she searched the house and gardens. She was
in equal measure distressed and suspicious, but she did
not, at first, suspect MacDougall for he told her the bare-
faced lie:

'Why, Mrs Hamilton, I saw the little chap snuffling
and scratching by the back gate, not ten minutes since,'
he said to her, and all the while stroking his fine gingery
moustaches.

'Ooohhhh! Lord!' she said to him, imagining what she
thought to be the worst.

The Mrs in Mrs Hamilton was a courtesy title, she had
never to my knowledge been married. She had a face like
a dromedary and voluminous skirts. I thought a lot about

her legs and imagined them to be exceptionally thick and sturdy. Probably of uniform diameter from top to bottom and ending in small casters rather than feet. Anywise, having been misdirected by the Doc, she trundled off to search first the street, and then the neighbourhood. At that point in time, Butty was in fact already stashed in the cellar and muzzled to prevent him barking for help. Of course, later, Mrs Hamilton discovered Doc MacDougall to be a liar and a poisoner, and she left his employ in high dudgeon.

That evening, we set to with the unfortunate pug. It was not anything a man could be proud of. Not even for science. First, he was quietened with an injection; a chemical concoction of the Doc's own devising, then a second injection was administered, which stopped the heart, killing the little brute stone dead. And all the while we had him suspended on a scale to measure his weight both alive and then dead and all the moments in between. As with the human subjects we had previously experimented upon, we boasted an accuracy in our measurements of one-sixteenth of an ounce. With hindsight, I might surmise that one-sixteenth to be the approximate weight of my self-respect. Would that I could claim the Doc's moral scruple to be so heavy.

Doc MacDougall reckoned on calculating the weight of the soul.

It was his overriding fixation that would brook no refute or counter. That man has a soul is a given, yet a cadaver may be opened and no evidence of it discovered. As far back as Andreas Vesalius, anatomists had failed to find evidence that may be extirpated and preserved, perhaps in a jar of formaldehyde like a gherkin. The obvious conclusion, posited MacDougal, is that before ever the scalpel opens the body, the soul has *already* departed.

Now the Doc had previously conducted experiments with actual persons dying from debilitating disease such as diabetes and tuberculosis. By persuasive argument or persistent bullshit, he obtained their written consent to observe and weigh them at the very instant of their passing, to determine if upon their expiration, something, *something* departed the body, leaving it some parts of an ounce lighter. Other so-called experts argued that a soul is immeasurable, like an ether, having neither mass nor weight. Mass and weight are not necessary to convince us of the existence of time, or gravity, or the colour blue. Sunlight is measurable in its increase and diminution, but not in ounces. Madness cannot be weighed, yet it exists, believe me.

Anyhow, Doc was evangelical in his research, but his results on those actual persons were shaky. Of six case studies, two were discounted for timing issues and apparatus malfunction, one was contra-indicative, one inconclusive, one fully supported, and one weakly supported the hypothesis. But the Doc was bullish. He was bullish by nature and intended to buttress the results by showing that whilst man, or even presumably woman, lost an average of eleven-sixteenths of an ounce when they passed, a dog would lose nothing because a dog has no soul. Of course, *you* are not a stupid person, *you* are not a pig-headed egomaniac, *you* will see at once that this is a complete non-sequitur and proves diddly-squat, but the Doc was suffering from tunnel vision on this point, and he was adamant that the evidence could be found, or made, or made to fit.

In his own words, it was 'not his fortune' to get dogs dying from such sickness as carried off the human subjects. Nor could he have gotten the dog's consent; why, those dogs knew even less of this fiasco than the old codgers he had cozened to sign his forms. So, the dogs, to put it plainly, were murdered.

'Samuel,' he said, 'when you have done with your inky splotches, be a good chap and dispose of the... er... remains. Wouldn't want Mrs Hamilton to... ah... stumble across...' And he flapped his hand as if the very words gave off a stink of death. So, after I had recorded the weights of Butterball the pug in the ledger, I began the grisly business of disposing of the body. I put it in a sack, left it outside the door, and went to wash my hands. I ran water into the basin and lathered my hands with soap. As I rinsed, I noticed that my signet ring had slipped off. I fished it from the water and put it back on my finger, but it wouldn't fit tight. My fingers seemed thinner, twig-like, and the ring kept slipping off, so I pocketed it for safe-keeping. It was a family heirloom and of sentimental value. The following day, the Doc went to the pound and came back with a fine spaniel and an old dog of no particular breed.

Whilst dealing with the mortal remains of the spaniel, I chanced to put my fingers to my collar and found it gaping wide around a newly scrawny neck. Since adolescence, I had always taken a fourteen-and-a-half-inch collar and I was certain it had fitted well that morning; I quite clearly recollected standing at the glass adjusting the studs. I put my hands around my throat as if to throttle myself; normally, the span of my fingers would barely contain the circumference. But now, my neck must be no more than eleven inches. Puzzling over this, I stroked the dog's fine silken chestnut coat and carried him out to the yard. As I moved him, his body sighed, and piss ran out onto my shoe. I have little inclination to dwell on that.

Next morning, I woke feeling shivery with my joints aching, as if with the onset of influenza, and found that in the night more reductions had taken place and my trousers no longer fitted. I rolled up the bottoms by about two-and-a-half inches and wore a pair of suspenders to keep them up. Gazing in the glass, which now seemed higher up the wall than before, I saw the usual face gazing back. The same old chin and throat, the same whiskers in whitish badger stripes with darker bristles between. Was I getting sick?

'You are late,' said Doc.

I checked my pocket watch and found he was right. My eighteen-minute walk to the surgery had taken twenty-one minutes and I was, in fact, tardy by those three minutes.

'It won't do, Samuel,' he said. 'It just won't do at all.'

He leaned back in his swivel chair with his button-booted feet on the desk, sipping at a cup of coffee. I was surprised that he did not comment upon my reduced stature, or indeed on my clownish trouser turn-ups but I guess he was, as usual, preoccupied with greater things, like punctuality.

This chastisement was interrupted by a knock at the door, and on attending, I found a down-at-heel gentleman and two lurchers on the step.

'They say yous is looking for dogs,' said the man.

He grabbed one of the lurchers by the muzzle and showed me its teeth which were in good order and the dog complained only a little at the handling.

'Wait,' I instructed and went to consult with MacDougall.

MacDougall quizzed the man briefly, then bought the dogs for a sum approximately one-fifth of the original asking price and they were kept in the back yard whilst he attended to his human patients. And then that evening, those two lurchers were co-opted into the mysteries of scientific research. The following morning, I had lost a further four-and-a-quarter inches in height.

I grew to loathe the very sight of the canine dispatching apparatus. A cage on a board, suspended by chains from the beam of a weighing scale. On the opposite side of the balance, a steel pan holding weights in stacks of pounds, topped by smaller weights for ounces and then a pyramid of finer weights for the parts of an ounce: a half, a quarter, an eighth, a sixteenth. First the board, cage, and sacking within were weighed and tabulated, then the dog would be added causing the beam to sway madly until the sedative took effect and the weight of the quiet dog could be calculated. Then came the killing. Before, and during, and for thirty minutes after death we watched for fluctuation in the weight of the subject. All the while, Doc was pontificating about the implications of heat exchange, evaporation and cooling, and one after another, all the dogs were weighing just the same dead as they had alive. I felt disheartened for the sake of the dogs that had given their lives for science. Doc had no such qualms.

'Do you see my boy?' he hooted, and he slapped my back. 'It is becoming a proven thing, Samuel. Proven. My earlier experiments are validated. No weight loss equals no soul. Dogs,' he said, 'dogs, my boy. Dogs have no soul.'

Another three dogs later, poisoned, weighed as they lay dying, and the balance arm unmoved by their departing this life, I had become so reduced that I was forced to buy new trousers and new shoes, both from the children's department of Lemuel Weeks & Co. I felt shamed in making these purchases, but I needed to be clothed and I consoled myself that at least I wasn't reduced to wearing doll's clothes. I was at that point the height and build of a seven-year-old but greying and sporting a full spade beard. Out in the streets I was jeered at, and boys threw sticks at me. My manly appetites remained undiminished.

The dog that grieved me most sorely was the last of the

fifteen. A white terrier bitch, the spit of Sue, a dog my grandparents had when I was a boy. When this little bitch came trotting obediently into the killing room, her tail fluffed out and her expression one of expectation, I thought my own small, sorry heart may well stop.

'Set to, set to, Samuel!' urged MacDougall, and he began to ready his bottles of sedatives and poisons and the syringes to administer them.

I fiddled with the paperwork. I refilled my pen. I could hardly bring myself to look at the dog, but when I did, I could see that she was a fair age and had had many litters. Her dugs were elongated and drooping, dark against the whitish fur of her undercarriage. She had probably suckled many cheerful and lusty pups in her time, and now she was come to this end. She was a small dog but quite stout and the Doc had to lift her to the scale as I was unable to muster the requisite strength.

'Quintessentially,' said Doc MacDougall, fingering his moustaches. 'Quintessentially, my boy, you increasingly prove yourself to be inept.'

My ineptitude was the only thing about me to be on the increase. I was so shortened, I could no longer see my face in the mirror above the sink, and I availed myself of a small folding stepladder from the janitor's cupboard, which I carried about under my arm. It was poor consolation, but after an alarmingly shaky start of random losses to various bodily dimensions, my shrinkage was progressing in a uniform manner so that though small, and getting smaller, I was at least all in proportion.

With the dog in position on the weighing apparatus, we went about the now routine business. The dog looked me steadily in the eye, unblinking and stoic when her end came, and I was overcome with shame and remorse. Yet still, I played my part in the recording of the weights. And when it was over, and the scale was lowered, I buried my face in the fur of her flank and I stroked her muzzle and wetted the brave girl with my tears and my snot.

I left the Doc's employ the next day. Like Mrs Hamilton, whose legs I still thought of frequently, I quit without notice. He still had said nothing about my much-reduced stature but was evidently put out that I was unable to perform many of my customary duties. I had not the strength, or I could not reach, and the Doc was having to do his own heavy lifting in more ways than just metaphorical. With each dog's passing my substance had diminished. I had lost not fractions or ounces per dog, but many pounds, and with no sign of it stopping.

Not knowing if I would shrink further, maybe to the size of a finger or a cricket or a pin head, I wrote to my younger brother telling him of my condition and enclosing uncle Zeb's signet ring so it might continue its journey through generations of our family. I had no option but to consider, at this juncture, that due to the shrinkage of my Johnson to around five-eighths of an inch, it was most unlikely that I would ever penetrate the mysteries of skirts, and father any children.

The pen was unwieldy to handle by then, so I wrote also my final goodbyes, sealed the envelope, and accepted help to put the letter onto the mail office counter. Mrs Mulligan took my letter and franked it. She offered to weigh me on her parcel scales, but I declined. She is a fine woman, Mrs Mulligan, and I had given a deal of thought to her legs. I imagined something of precision engineering with hinges and a system of hydraulics enabling her to be so flexible and efficient.

Walking home from the mail office, trying to avoid getting bowled over or trodden on, I conjectured that I might shrink so much as to pass under the hems of skirts without notice, and so have the opportunity to admire a great many ladies' fine legs, to examine their construction, and observe their primary and ancillary functions. Rather disturbingly, as I shrunk in stature, I was becoming more horny, as if my natural manly inclinations had become condensed or distilled, less in volume but of greater proof.

I was acutely aware of being a curiosity. In point of fact, I wondered about seeking alternative employment in a travelling fair or freak show, but I was uneasy about mingling with rough, circus-bred types. The prospect of being gawped at was unsavoury, and besides, the very idea of man's exploitation of lesser beings by either the payment or the collection of a nickel was anathema to me. So, I determined to forgo the dubious excitement of the travelling show and live out my days as quietly as I might. To that end, I have become reclusive, concealing myself as much as possible from the natural curiosity of others and abjuring all company. Children in particular can be very direct. Very cruel.

I live now in a small hut in the grounds of an empty house, at the far end of Warwick Street. It would be some kind of justice if I made my home in a kennel, but truth be told, it used to be a chicken coop. Being no taller than a bantam rooster, it is sufficient. The big house is all locked up and I do not venture to sneak in through some small crevice, but content myself with the gardens which provide for many of my needs. There is an abundance of fruit bushes, and earthworms, which are easily digested. I have few possessions left; my shrinkage has obviated the need for much that I previously considered important. My old pocket watch I have kept, and though its face is now near as big as my own, I find its constant tick a comfort while I sleep. I don't honestly know how much longer this life is sustainable; since the end of my involvement in Doc MacDougal's crazy experimentations, the rate of my decline has slowed, but it has not altogether stopped.

I believe I will ready soon, to slip through.

The Not So Funny Man

By Deirdre Crowley

Deirdre Crowley is and artist and writer from Bandon Co. Cork, Ireland. Her stories have been published in The Irish Times, The Ogham Stone, The Southern Star, and The Well Short Story Competition. In 2017, she was one of twelve writers short listed for The Sunday Business Post Short Story Award Short. In 2018 she was longlisted for FISH Memoir Prize. In 2019 she was selected for Cork World Book Festival Pitch with an Agent event. In the same year her work was Longlisted and Highly Commended in the Sean O Faolin Short Story Contest.

Last night I dreamt that there was a black horse in my bed. It is a single bed these days by the way, like all the other ones here. Sometimes I try not to remember my dreams, but this one seemed okay. The black horse kept on standing up, repositioning himself and lying down again, as if he was figuring out what was most comfortable. I was standing next to him wondering why he seemed to like putting his silky mane on the three pillows I usually slept on. I was thinking, *Surely that cannot be comfortable for him with his long neck*, but this horse did not seem to mind. I did not intervene with suggestions to him. Once he had settled, he looked like he would start reading one of the books near my reading lamp. I could hardly ask him to leave; he looked so comfortable. Maybe he was the kind of horse who liked to read in bed just like me.

The dream reminded me of my dog, the way she used to love to jump up on my double bed when we lived in the cottage. I loved my dog, but I drew the line at her being in my bed or on my bed. (She was half collie and half something else smart. We had chosen each other at the rescue centre. We both had wanted a new life.) The only time I would have made an exception to the rule was the night The Not So Funny Man came to stay at my house. I had not invited him; he just seemed to arrive. I had met him and his friend, The Funny One, on a train journey that summer. I was sitting at one of those four seats with a table. I had wanted to sleep and not talk to anyone, but when the train broke down halfway into our journey, conversation started automatically and never stopped for the next hour. The Funny One made me laugh a lot. He had been an actor when younger and now wrote plays for his local dramatic company. They were travelling home after the funeral of a classmate. Arriving at my destination, mobile numbers were exchanged only out of politeness.

'If you're ever up our way,' The Funny One said. 'Me and my wife will treat you to afternoon tea, nothing fancy, just a bit of china and theatrics.'

It all seemed quite harmless. The Not So Funny One insisted on carrying my bag off the train. Other passengers looked at me disapprovingly. A peck on the cheek from both men on the platform must have seemed like I was saying goodbye to my two grandfathers.

Weeks later The Not So Funny One phoned me to tell me that his brother had died. I offered my sympathy. He went on to explain how his brother's wife had shut him out. He said that she would not allow him say goodbye to his brother. I remembered how on the train The Funny One had confided in me that The Not So Funny One had a very bitter split from his wife, and how none of his children spoke to him anymore. Just as he was about to say more, The Not so Funny One came back from the buffet carriage with drinks and chocolate. Maybe if The Funny One had been able to tell me more, I would have acted differently.

The next phone call I got from the Not So Funny one, was late one gloomy September evening. He said he was in the area and would it be okay if he called to say hello. I was surprised that he had remembered where I lived. As part of the conversation on the train, I had told them that I lived near a tiny village close to the sea. At the time neither of them seemed to know of it. They both lived over a hundred kilometres away. We may as well have been living in different countries.

'I'm really tired, I can only stay a while,' he seemed to be whispering wearily down the phone.

I stuttered that I might be going out, but realised it was too late. He had hung up.

I had barely time to put on my shoes and jumper when I heard a car crunch onto the gravel. I wondered how he had found me so easily without me giving clear directions. Visitors usually got lost, even with my detailed advice on how to get to me. The twisty roads and turnoffs were easily confused, especially in the dark. I got lost myself some nights.

I opened the glass porch door, as the car headlights dazzled me and my dog. She was barking, instantly annoyed at his arrival. He got out of the car quickly, his eyes shining wildly, his white hair dishevelled and wiry. He looked like someone I had seen in a play once, his bony features waxy from the sensor light.

He opened the back door of the car, taking out flowers and a parcel wrapped in brown paper. On the threshold he presented them to me saying,

'Now, girl, they're for you.' The way he said 'girl' made me shiver. Rolling the word slowly off his tongue, he made it sound vulgar. Walking past me he went for the kitchen, like he knew where it was. He seemed to be moving faster than I had remembered. I paused at the door, feeling like someone was trespassing; it took me a while to follow him into the kitchen. I offered him tea as he walked around admiring everything and me.

'It's so good to see you,' he said, squeezing my shoulders as I filled the kettle in the sink. His fingers felt claw-like, his breath sounded heavy near my neck.

'Ouch!' he shouted. 'You little bitch.'

My dog had nipped him on the heel.

I apologised and gave a pretend scold to my dog who was panting at my knee. She was doing her stressed yawning, something I saw her do rarely. It usually happened at the vets, or if we were in places that were too crowded or around people she thought too loud. She was standing rigid next to me like she was stuck in cement. When he turned his back, I rubbed her ear. She licked my sweaty wrist, yet neither of us relaxed.

'I'm exhausted,' The Not So Funny Man said, flattening his thin hair down as he sat at the kitchen table. Stretching out his long legs and exposing bare hairy ankles, he was sockless in his polished brown brogues. His laces were untied too.

He glanced quickly over his shoulders as if checking to see if anyone might be listening.

'I don't think I can drive home tonight. I just might stay here,' he said emphatically. 'I haven't been sleeping well, you know!'

He was bowing his head now over his cup. His hands seemed to tremble as he held the steaming tea. This gesture made him seem smaller, almost vulnerable. His eyes looked bloodshot. It had not occurred to me that he might have been drinking.

'I know it's late,' he said. 'It is so nice to see you, and I can see you are happy to see me too.' He licked his lips and nodded as if agreeing with himself.

'That's it decided then, I'll stay tonight and be gone first thing in the morning.'

He was staring at me now, his look intimidating.

'Yes, yes of course,' I said far too quickly. 'I have a spare room for visitors.'

I really wanted to add that usually my visitors were invited and did not just land out of nowhere in the dark and that my dog had never nipped anyone before, not even the postman.

I poured more tea from the white ceramic tea pot I had bought when I moved into the cottage. It was a symbol of my new clean life. I had hoped that I might become a minimalist someday, with everything white and tidy. I had rented the place on my own after two break-ups. One was devastating and the other just another mistake. Initially the

cottage had given me time to heal, but recently I was glad
I had only signed a one-year lease. I did not know how I
would survive a winter there. There were too many crows in
the trees nearby. Sometimes it seemed that collectively they
could block out the sky. Other times they made so much
noise I had to keep the windows shut. Lately I could hear
them cawing in my head, even when sleeping.

The Not So Funny Man was smiling at me now. He
seemed to be about to reach out and touch me.

'I've run out of milk,' I said in a panic, jumping up
quickly. My dog moved with me. The thought of having to
talk to him for longer was making me queasy.

'I'll drive to the village,' he said, clapping his hands.

'In fact, we can both go and have a drink in the pub while
we're there. It is a nice little pub. They know all about you
there.'

I felt myself go hotter. I had never been in the local pub;
there were always men outside smoking. They would stare
at my car as I drove past, early or late, it did not matter.
At weekends, teenage girls in short dresses and young
boys in T-shirts huddled around the entrance smoking
and laughing, waiting for the bus to take them to the
neighbouring town nightclub. Sometimes one or two would
be vomiting at the side entrance under the yard light. On
Sunday mornings there were always plastic glasses and chip
wrappers blowing around the road like tattered ghosts from
the night before. The woman who ran the pub had dyed
black frizzy hair and big teeth. I would see her standing
in the door with the smoking men and teenagers laughing
one minute, glaring at passing traffic the next. She always
seemed to be wearing white jeans and tops. I wondered
how she would keep them clean if she was pulling pints.
Maybe someone else was doing that for her. The girl in the
shop said she was great for the village. She said if it wasn't

for her they would have nothing, especially the teenagers, they had nowhere else to go.

That place was the last place I wanted to go.

'No, no,' I replied. 'You stay here, and I'll be back in no time.'

'Don't worry,' he said. 'We don't need to go to the pub, I have a bottle of wine in the car for you too. I'll wait until you come back to open it.'

'No,' I insisted. 'I don't drink wine.'

I had not taken a drink in a long time. It was my way of breaking from the habits that in the past had made me fall. I had lost friends because I did not like drinking anymore.

'You're not much fun,' one friend said.

'You've just become boring,' another scolded.

I did not know which was better, having friends like that who told you exactly what they thought, or getting rid of friends like that. It was hard to accept that people I had liked once no longer wanted to be with me.

I gathered my coat and bag and went to leave. I could not find my phone. I was convinced I had left it in the kitchen. It did not seem to matter now that I was getting away from The Not So Funny Man. He stood at the door waving. 'Don't be long now, we'll have a nice chat when you get back.'

Smiling, he closed the door.

My dog barked all the way to the village. She had never barked like that; being in the car was always something that she liked. It was nearly ten o clock; I knew the village shop would be closed. The woman from the bar stood in the doorway and gave me an unsettling wave as I drove by. What did she know about me, I wondered?

I drove on to the town, not sure where would be open, half convincing myself that I did need milk after all. It was comforting to be in a place with streetlights. I could call Yvonne, but she would probably be in bed with her

husband. She had visited me once or twice, but I had never
been officially invited back to her place. It was a Tuesday
night, a back-to-school feel made the poorly lit houses seem
joyless. What would I say to Yvonne anyway? There is an
old man staying in my house tonight and I am afraid to stay
there now?

Yvonne was a new friend that I had made at the weekly
farmers' market. The cakes and scones I baked were
popular with the Saturday shoppers. She made fudge; she
swore she never ate it herself as it was too sugary. The
other stall holders were less friendly. They viewed me with
suspicion. Most of them had authoritative accents that
sounded like they knew about everything. They would talk
to each other loudly in between customers. When we were
packing up later, Yvonne and I would laugh at some of the
things they would say.

'Where are you from?' the guy from the buffalo
mozzarella stall had asked me my first day.

'From out the road,' I replied. 'Ten miles away.'

'Ah, but you're not really from here,' he said. 'You're not
local.' He kept on at me, joking yet serious.

He claimed he was local because he had lived in the town
for three years.

Yvonne said he was hitting on me. She said he had tried
the same tactics with her until he saw her husband. She was
convinced he had army background. She said that the knife
and boots were a dead giveaway. She accused me of being
too shy for my own good. It was something I could not help.

The woman selling organic honey had quizzed me about
who had recommended me to the committee of the farmers'
market. She asked me where I had trained. I told her that
my grandmother had taught me how to bake. Foolishly,
I found myself telling her about how she had raised me
too. I do not know why I gave her that information, I must

have been nervous. She did not seem remotely interested but raved on about Imelda's cakes next to her stall, telling me that they were all gluten free and organic. Imelda just glared at me. She looked like the least organic person you could imagine. Her face was orange. I wondered if organic carrots made you go that colour. I had read once that carotene was a natural tanning agent.

It was drizzling now as I circled the town looking to see if anywhere was open. My dog had settled down, and in the mirror I could see her attempting to sleep. I felt drowsy myself. I pulled into the church carpark. Surely with the doors locked we would be safe parked up there for the night? The graveyard residents nearby would keep watch over us.

Then I remembered something my grandmother used to say, it was that a kindness to a stranger could save a life. Why was I being so foolish? The man in my house was only a few years younger than my grandmother had been when she died. I was with her holding her hand. When I had to let it go finally, I remember feeling abandoned for the first time in my twenty-five years of living. Now years later I felt the same aloneness, it came down around me heavy as the dark. I had to push the weight off as a pain dragged across my chest. Deep breathing, I reasoned with myself that the best thing to do would be to head back to the cottage. I had to be up early in the morning to do an order of cakes for a birthday party. My dog would get to sleep on my bed for one night only. Everything would be fine.

Approaching the village, I noticed a dead badger, blood and fur squashed into the ground; further up the road, a headless pigeon. I had not seen these casualties earlier. They were not unusual around here. As the car crawled slowly up the hill to the cottage, my dog awoke and started barking again. The light was on in the guest bedroom, the curtains were pulled, his car was gone though; I felt relief.

Entering the cottage, a strange musty smell hung in the air. On the kitchen table a bottle of red wine stood open alongside a drained glass. Lifting it, I inhaled the bitter aroma. It was almost empty. My phone lay there, the screen dead to touch. Walking down the hall, I stopped when I got to the guest room. I knocked on the bedroom door and called out. I turned the silver handle, opening it slowly. The bedclothes looked dented. He must have slept for a while and then left. That was all he had wanted, I told myself. Now I worried if he had been fit to drive. I started to shake the pillows and smooth the covers. My dog shot hurriedly to the porch door, scratching it wildly to get out. I followed her. The barking was piercing until I screamed at her to stop. When I opened the door, The Not So Funny Man was standing there saying,

'Where have you been, my love, don't you know I've been waiting all night for you?'

Red wine dripped from his bloodied lips. His wet body raged toward me. Everything went dark. Even the crows were silent, just like me.

Her

By Alison Nuorto

An EFL Teacher living in Bournemouth but with a nomadic heart that yearns to roam far and wide. She feasts on horror stories and the traditional ghost stories of M.R.James and harbours an appreciation for the macabre. Her poems have appeared in a handful of anthologies and she was delighted to make the shortlist for the Bournemouth Writing Prize in 2021. Currently, she is working on producing an anthology of her own to promote awareness of male suicide. As long as she has a pulse, she hopes to always keep writing.

'So...' Mark hesitated before looking down. 'Who's this new man your mum's been seeing?'

'Oh, Rupert? He's great.' Jake replied, immediately toning down his enthusiasm upon spotting Mark's hurt expression.

'Rupert? That's a posh name, isn't it?' Mark exclaimed, not meaning to sound quite so jealous.

'Err, I guess so. Haven't really thought about it to be honest,' Jake replied, attempting to sound nonchalant. 'Well, we're both really excited about Bali.' Jake brightened. 'Mum's been buying loads of dresses. I bet she doesn't end up wearing half of them'.

'Bali? He's taking you to Bali?' Mark felt a sharp twinge in his chest.

'Yes, for two weeks. Oh Dad, I thought Mum had told you.'

The flash bastard, Mark thought to himself. The only place he'd ever managed to take them, was to his Uncle Graham's mobile home in Dorset.

'It must be getting serious then,' Mark said softly, almost in a whisper.

'Well, he is round a lot but Mum doesn't want him to move in as yet. She wants to make sure that we're both comfortable with it first.

There was that sharp twinge again.

'So, why is he taking you both on holiday?' Inwardly, Mark prayed that this Rupert character wasn't intending to propose.

'He said it's a treat to celebrate my GCSE results.'

'I'm so proud of you son.' Mark instinctively ruffled Jake's hair, which clearly embarrassed him. 'I always knew you were bright. You definitely got your brains from your mum.'

'Thanks, Dad,' Jake smiled.

Mark suddenly brightened. 'How about we plan a trip away? Just the two of us – father and son. Anywhere you like.'

'That sounds great, Dad. Yeah, let's do that.' Jake patted his father's shoulder reassuringly.

'Look, Jake... I know I've said it before but I'm sorry. I really am sorry.' Mark gazed into his son's eyes, as his eyes watered.

'It's okay, Dad. I understand.'

Mark acknowledged just how mature Jake was for his age. Far more sensible than he'd ever been, even as an adult. He really didn't deserve such a good son. He felt the sting of guilt every time he looked at this handsome, intelligent and level-headed young man before him. His son was from a broken home because of his mistake. He'd given into temptation and his momentary lapse of judgement had ruptured what had been a solid and happy marriage. His ex-wife only allowed him to see Jake on a whim when it suited her. He couldn't protest because she'd been granted full custody. Now, some posh, loaded, cocky interloper had usurped his place at the table – and in his bed.

'Dad, you've lost weight and you're looking a bit gaunt. You're not ill, are you?' Jake looked concerned.

'No, I'm fine, son. Just haven't been sleeping well. I think I'm just run-down.'

'Are you eating properly? You've definitely lost weight.'

Mark laughed. 'Who's the father here? It's okay, I'm fine really. Don't worry.'

Jake smiled half-heartedly.

'Your mum... Is she happy?' Mark asked tentatively, after a brief silence.

Jake shifted in his seat. 'She was happy with you, Dad ... but yes, she seems happy.'

Mark remembered when he and Jake's mum, Shelley, really had been happy. Childhood sweethearts, on their second day at primary school, she'd splashed his face with blue paint. When she saw her handiwork, she painted her own nose blue, so they would match.

This gesture made him vow to follow this angelic, slightly clumsy, red-haired beauty anywhere. They'd struggled financially after Jake was born, but they'd always been on the same page, and were determined to give him the best education they could provide. Their situation began to improve when he'd secured a pay rise, and Shelley was embarking on setting up her own mobile beauty business. They hadn't been able to afford a holiday abroad, but his dream of a fly-drive holiday to the States, was tantalisingly close to being realised. During a quiet lull in the office, he would close his eyes and imagine their beaming faces as they tore along Route 66 in the American sunshine.

That was before his moment of weakness drove a giant wedge between them. They had stayed together – for Jake – but Shelley had struggled to contain her resentment and anger. How could he blame her? Their robotic love-making destroyed them both.

'I can't get her out of my head. When we're intimate, I wonder if you're thinking about her, if it's her you see when you're kissing me… touching me. She's always going to be a spectre, haunting this marriage.'

There was nothing that Mark could say to that. Silence seemed preferable to feeble protestations.

'I still love you,' she'd said one evening, after one of their habitual arguments. 'But the respect has gone,' she'd added sadly.

Mark looked at Jake affectionately. He felt heartened by his son's concern for his well-being. He was reluctant to reveal the reason behind his poor sleep quality. The nightmares had started up again. The guilt-fuelled dreams that had started just before he and Shelley had decided to part ways. He'd wake up shaking and drenched in sweat. It was a detail that he'd intentionally kept from his son. He'd always slept poorly, so Jake hadn't pressed him further. The nightmares were so vivid and realistic, they were almost an accurate account of his act of foolishness.

It was an unusually warm afternoon in April. He had the day off and was on his way to collect Jake from school. He'd decided to stop and get some roses for Shelley as a surprise. Waiting in line at the florists, he couldn't help but notice the young girl in front of him. He guessed that she was about twenty-one. Her waist-length, blonde hair shimmered in the sunlight that streamed in, and he smelt a hint of apple and jasmine. She was wearing a maxi yellow sundress that made her behind look temptingly pinchable, he'd decided. He felt himself getting hard and held the roses strategically, so nobody would notice. He was so transfixed by her figure, he didn't notice when her transaction finished, and she turned around to catch him mid-ogle. He was mortified but she'd smiled, tilted her head to one side and run her long fingers through her tresses.

Back in the car, Mark was on cloud nine. He'd certainly enjoyed his encounter with the sexy nymph in the florists but he was also waiting on an important call from the office. Probably one of the most important calls of his life. He was up for promotion and his supervisor had promised to call him with the outcome before the end of the day. Based on the glowing feedback from his most recent appraisal, it seemed to be in the bag but still, Mark knew from experience never to count his chickens. He'd been on tenterhooks all day. Nothing but nervous energy – and, more recently, arousal. He checked his phone: no calls or messages.

When he stopped at the traffic lights, he spotted her. The temptress from the florists was waiting to cross. His eyes were roaming over her curves as his phone began vibrating furiously. Quickly looking to the screen, he saw that it was work. He should have ignored it but felt that it would make him look bad.

He answered just to let them know that he was driving and that he'd be home in ten minutes. His supervisor agreed and he promptly ended the call. In his nerve-fuelled haste, he neglected to check that the lights had changed. He was still looking down at his phone when he put his foot on the pedal. There was the most unnatural sound and he assumed that a tyre had blown out, until he recognized the Pre-Raphaelite tresses splayed across his windscreen and the flimsy summer dress that billowed across his bonnet like a sail.

'I have to go now, Dad. You will take care of yourself, won't you?'

Mark smiled grimly, nodding weakly.

'I'll visit again soon, I promise,' Jake added. 'I'll try to persuade Mum to come next time,' he called out hopefully, as an afterthought, as a guard ushered him out.

'Time, what a strange concept,' Mark pondered to himself. Some people would give their eye teeth to have more, while others have far too much. As for him, now, he had nothing but time.

A Good Boy

By Sam Szanto

Sam has had over 30 stories and poems published & listed in competitions. In 2021, she was a semi-finalist in the St Lawrence Book Awards, highly commended in Write by the Sea KQ, placed third in the Erewash Open Competition, longlisted for the Crowvus Ghost Competition, and published in Storgy, Personal-Bests Journal 3, Glittery Literary Anthology 2 and the Parracombe Prize Anthology. She won the 2020 Charroux Poetry Prize and the First Writer's Poetry Prize.

There was nothing exceptional about me until I had the operation. However, the day that I was born – 10th January 1946 – was special. Not because of my birth, which didn't affect many people, even my parents: they already had five kids. But thousands of miles away, while my mother was labouring to get me out of her body in Leeds General Infirmary, the US Army was bouncing a radar signal off the moon from Fort Monmouth, New Jersey. On the same day in London, the UN General Assembly was meeting for the first time. So, there was potency to that day.

You're interested in my birth? It wasn't particularly traumatic, as far as I know. People didn't talk about that type of thing in those days. I know Mam was in hospital for ten days; that was the norm then. I wish I could remember when I was the most important thing in her life. I imagine her smiling down at me, tired but happy. While the US Army Signal Corps was trying its best to probe another celestial body and fifty-one nations were stuffing themselves into the Methodist Central Hall in London, all Mary West was interested in was the beauty of her sixth-born child. Maybe. There are no photos from that time.

And then, once those possibly blissful ten days were over, the reality. Mam and I went home. To my father, who I'll tell you about later. To my siblings: ten, eight, seven, five and three years old; Susan, Mickey, Jennifer, Bill and Evie: only Jennifer is alive now. I wasn't the last child my parents had: two years' after me, Albie came along. We squashed into a flat on the seventh storey of a block in Quarry Hill; destroyed now. Mam spent most of her time cooking and cleaning. The older kids played with the younger ones, helped them with getting dressed and all the rest of it. I got a rudimentary education: it wasn't compulsory for parents to send kids to school until 1948, so my four eldest siblings had less schooling than me. I was clever, so found school okay. I especially enjoyed the teachers reading to us and singing songs. At break-times there was milk, although on cold days their ice-collars made it difficult to stuff the straws in. In the summer, the liquid curdled before the teachers got the bottles into the classroom. But in the spring and autumn, the milk was good.

You want to know about my father, of course. He worked as a smith, and drank most of his wages away. Same as so many men who'd survived the war. In the late 1940s, there weren't SSRIs or talking therapies. There was alcohol. It chased away the memories, I suppose.

Was he scary? He came home slurring, and his slurs struck the night. Sometimes we kids would run out of the backdoor. We'd come home a few hours later, hungry and cold. Evie once told a teacher about Dad hitting Mam, but she was told not to tell wicked lies or would go to hell.

As I got older, Mam got a broken arm and severe concussion. At the hospital, she said she slipped. I began to worry that he would kill her. Mam was a skinny woman and no more than five feet tall. Dad was six foot. Not right, is it, someone like that picking on a little woman like Mam, who had never done anything but protect him?

Some people think violence is hereditary, don't they? As a boy, I'd never hurt anyone beyond the normal rough play, but what Dad did to Mam made me so furious I wanted to smash my fist against his face, throw him out of our high window. But I wasn't strong enough, and he would kill me. I had to devise a plan to get rid of him.

My first idea was poisoning, and an idea quickly formed for how I could do it. My father hated flies so much that he kept fly-killer paper in the house. To my mind, my father was more dangerous than a little insect, and deserved to die more than one.

When he was at the pub, I got hold of his special Queen's Coronation mug and unearthed the flypaper. I would make my father a very special cuppa. The flypaper had a strong scent, and the fumes started to overwhelm me as I scraped the adhesive into the mug. Albie found me sleeping. He clipped me round the ear for my foolishness, even though he was younger than me.

'I've got a better idea, Stan,' he said.

Albie's idea was to loosen the carpet on the staircase, so that Dad tripped and broke his neck. He said he would do it but I told him it was my duty, the elder brother.

Dad caught me in the act. And that was where it all started.

'You used to be a good boy – what happened? Get out and don't come back.'

'Please no, Fred,' Mum said. 'He still is a good boy. It was one silly prank, wasn't it, Stan? You didn't want to seriously hurt anyone, did you?'

'Wake up, Mary! He was trying to kill me.'

'If you want someone to be angry at, Fred, be angry at me.'

'Be angry at me,' Albie shrieked. 'It wasn't Stan's idea, it was mine.'

My father raised his eyebrows, thick and heavy like slabs of meat. Then he raised his fist. I assume the only reason he didn't hit anyone was that he couldn't decide which of the three of us to whack.

'I'm going,' I said.

My mother and brother took it in turns to hug me. The hallway glittered as if washed in tears.

I spent my sixteenth birthday walking the streets, the open throat of the sky above me. Two months were spent sleeping in parks and shop doorways. I was spat at and pissed on, although sometimes drunks gave me the rest of their bottle or put a shilling in my hand.

I stole food to survive. Yes, that was how I ended up in Borstal. Was it awful? At least it was warm. We did sports, had lessons. Bit like school, the difference being that the pupils and teachers were terrifying, and we were locked in our cells on what felt like a whim. And there was no milk. My mum, weeping, came to visit, as did my siblings. Often Mum would have a black eye or a cut on her face.

I started getting headaches. They were hands squeezing my skull, as lights burst like stars behind my eyes. The air trembled. The doctor was fetched after I'd been shouting with pain for hours. I was put in a van and taken to hospital. Not a normal hospital; a psychiatric hospital. Yes, that one.

'I'm not mad,' I shouted when I found out where I was.

The next day I met Doctor Johns, the psychiatrist in charge of my case. You've done research on him, I know. Was he a monster? He didn't look like one, with his round-rimmed glasses and dapper suit, his permanent smile. His moustache made me think of the school milk, the competitions after drinking it to see who had the whitest top lip.

'We believe you have severe mental problems, Stanley.' Doctor Johns had an excited look on his face. 'Your father says you're very aggressive: you tried to kill him.'

'He's been trying to kill my mother for years,' I said.

'Don't worry, Stanley. All of this is treatable. We have wonderful medicines and therapies these days. You're in safe hands.'

Yes, he really said that.

The wonderful medicines were psychotropic drugs and electroconvulsive therapy sessions. The ECTs were like a hammer smashing against my skull, again and again. It made the headaches I had in Borstal feel like nothing.

Doctor Johns sat by my bed, smoothing the knees of his suit trousers. Smiling as always.

'Excellent news, Stanley,' he said.

'I can go home?' I was barely able to push out the words through the drug-fuzz. Did I have a home anymore? Had I stretched the bridge of my life so far that I could no longer cross it? Even being murdered by my father seemed a better alternative to the ECTs. I had had eight by then, and felt I knew what it was to be hit by a wrecking ball in the blind dark. When I could open my eyes afterwards, the bright light bit my retinas.

Doctor Johns frowned briefly before pasting on his smile again. 'Home? Oh no, Stanley. Your father is adamant that you can't return until you've been properly cured. He just wants you to be a good boy; it's all parents want for their children, isn't it? And I have a brilliant idea for what could enable that to happen. There is a little operation which I fervently – fervently, Stanley – believe would seriously alter your innate levels of aggression. Remove them entirely, perhaps.'

'No thanks,' I said, dribbling.

Doctor Johns' moustache drooped a little. 'The problem is, Stan – can I call you that? we're friends now – is that aggression gets worse if untreated. Imagine you get married – handsome boy like you, you'll have your pick – then you'll want children, won't you?'

I thought of my large family. All of us in the flat when Dad was down the pub, playing card games and laughing. Even Mum. I thought of Albie and I restoring a bike we'd found, polishing it and getting spare parts from the scrap yard; Jennifer teaching me chess; Mickey letting me go on his paper round and buying me sweets at the end.

'You wouldn't want to harm your own children, would you? We believe this operation will stop that happening.

You'll have a peaceful, easy life.'

Bells rang in my head.

'The procedure will mean pulling back the skin on your forehead before we drill two small holes into your skull,' Doctor Johns said cheerily. 'After that, a nylon ball will be inserted into each hole. It'll be over before you know it. It's an easy operation, no different from slicing through a block of cheese really – easier than curing toothache.'

'I don't want it,' I said. 'I'm not going to hurt my kids.'

'Your father has given permission,' Doctor Johns said, as if I hadn't spoken. Perhaps I hadn't. I was so woozy, it was hard to know what was happening. 'He clearly wants the best for his son. You're lucky; I couldn't stand my dad, ha ha.'

'What if I say no to the operation?'

'You're lucky to be in a position to have it. Special – the chosen one. Not many people have been cured the way you will be. Once it's over you won't go back to Borstal; you'll have your freedom.'

My mother had taught us to respect doctors. Perhaps I was aggressive. I had been in Borstal, and was the only one of my siblings to have been thrown out of the family home. I had tried to kill my father, twice.

'Good boy,' Doctor Johns said, touching my shoulder through the hospital gown.

One more smile, and he was gone. I watched the moon shine onto my bed. The stars, though, they sank down. And then it was dark, and I was left staring at the windows' empty eyes.

At four minutes past one in the afternoon, I was wheeled into an operating theatre.

I woke with swollen eyes, feeling bruised and nauseous. My face was wet with sweat. Sitting up, I was immediately sick on the bed clothes, to the disgust of the nurse who had to clean it up. There was a pain in my head that I can only liken to having a broom handle inserted repeatedly into my skull. My skin was burning. The feeling of my hospital gown where it touched my flesh was torture.

'It's going splendidly so far, Stanley.' Doctor Johns was the happiest I'd seen him. 'Your family won't recognise you.'

I could say nothing.

'You're in illustrious company, did you know that? Lenin and Einstein both had their brains scrutinised. Einstein's was kept in mayonnaise jars and given to friends by his pathologist. Can you imagine that?'

Can *you* imagine that?

'We should see a complete difference after the next stage,' Doctor Johns said. 'You'll be put under your old angry self, then when we wake you up – new Stanley. Like turning a coin over: bad boy on one side, good boy on the other.'

The second stage lasted for nearly nine hours; a long time to turn a coin over. I was awake, strapped down, the doctors watching as my pupils dilated.

The surgery involved electrodes being placed into my hypothalamus, then they shot volts through the electrodes into my brain.

Want to have a break? Well, if you're sure, I'll carry on. Visiting time is limited.

So, back to the op. I screamed and screamed throughout. I have had flashbacks of that surgery every day for the past fifty-six years; nightmares every night.

It was all good from Doctor Johns' point of view.

'Calm down, son,' he said, smiling as always as I screamed. 'Thought Borstal kids were tougher than this.'

I emerged from the operation in a stupor, incontinent

and unaware of who I was or what had happened to me. I was an empty country, the other inhabitants having fled when the looters and pillagers arrived.

My mother and siblings visited. Mam took my hand and said something, but I didn't understand. Words swallowed themselves on my lips, time after time. They sizzled like the wings of moths. I lay back on my pillows and closed my eyes. I felt my hands being gently squeezed, heard whispered goodbyes.

Eight days later, I was told I could go, the plastic balls still sticking out of my forehead. As they thought I had been cured of my natural aggressive tendencies, I was permitted to go home, although I didn't know how I would get there. My family were all at work or school. Even Mam had a job now, in a clothing factory, Dad having been laid off. He was trying to borrow a friend's car to pick me up, was the message I received from Mam. But on the day of my discharge, I didn't know if he had been successful, and resigned myself to taking two buses.

I walked out of the hospital into a mid-winter city which was virtually silent. My legs were like cotton wool and my head screamed with pain. I carried my bag on my back, and even though I had little inside it, it felt as though I were carrying my coffin.

I made my slow way to the bus stop. There were a few old people waiting, all of whom stared in horror as I approached. I touched the plastic balls on my forehead and lowered my head. Gazed at the few cars prowling past.

In a blaze of light, a bus arrived. I waited for the old people to make their way onto it; none of them thanked me, all avoided meeting my eye. As I effortfully climbed the step, I realised I had no money for a fare. I tried to explain to the bus driver that I'd just come out of hospital, had no money, would I be able to have one free ride? I'll get the money to the bus company afterwards, I said. He shook his head. Everyone on the bus was watching me.

I got off the bus without arguing and sat at the stop, leaning my head against the cool plastic. I was so tired my eyes began to close.

When I woke, it was dark. There was no one at the bus stop. I got up and saw that the road and house tops had an icy sheen. I didn't feel cold, which seemed strange. I didn't realise then that the operation had affected my ability to feel temperatures appropriately.

Suddenly a car was heading down the road towards me, travelling too fast. In an almost balletic movement, it glided off the road. Skidded on a patch of ice, I suppose. It narrowly avoided crashing into the bus shelter.

Dad got out of the car and walked towards me, seemingly unharmed by the crash. Of course he was; nothing touched him.

As he got closer, his smile froze.

I don't get many visitors in here, and I was worried when you approached me. I trust so few people these days, especially those I don't know. Few people have had my experience, so I don't expect understanding; just an audience.

Black Snow

By EJ Robinson

EJ Robinson is a writer and tour guide based in London. Her work has been shortlisted for the Wicked Young Writers' Award and the Exeter Short Story Competition, and published in numerous magazines and anthologies.

The dwarves found her asleep in the longest bed: a girl child with white skin stained with forest floor dirt, and black hair that flowed across the pillow to cascade down the bedside. When the girl awoke, she started back against the head of the bed at the sight of seven little men, but the dwarves held up fourteen rough palms.

'We mean you no harm, young girl,' they said.

The girl told the men how she had come to be in their cottage. How her wicked stepmother had ordered a huntsman to take her deep into the forest and leave her there as food for the wolves. When she realised his intention, she leapt from his horse and ran. She kept on running until she glimpsed a cottage through the trees, whereupon she collapsed from exhaustion and terror. She dabbed the coverlet to the corners of her eyes as she told her story. The dwarves gathered about her.

'There, there,' they said. 'Have no fear. You may shelter with us.'

'You'd do that for me? You don't know me,' said the girl.

'In return for shelter you may do our cooking and cleaning and gardening for us. We're seven working men, we've been needing a woman around the house.'

'I shall gladly do anything you need,' said the girl. And she told them her name. It was Snow White.

'Miss White, we live in the middle of a deep, dark forest. There are many strange creatures and people lurking within it who may wish to do a young girl like you harm. Everyday we go to work in the diamond mines, and you will be left in the cottage alone. As you go about your work for us, never answer the door to strangers. They might be dangerous.'

'Strangers can indeed be dangerous,' Snow said, glancing at a shelf above the kitchen window.

'Yes, they can,' said the dwarves. 'So promise us, Miss White. Promise that you will never ever answer the door to strangers.'

'I promise,' said Snow.

The next morning Snow rose early while the seven little men snored in their beds. She swept out the rooms, she dusted the furniture, she trimmed the wicks in the oil lamps. She discovered blue tits and pigeons nesting in the eaves, speckled eggs snuggled up against their warm breasts. She found families of voles and rabbits living deep within the kitchen cupboards.

'How adorable you all are,' said Snow. 'Don't be frightened, little ones. I'm just here to look after the seven men in return for their kindness in letting me stay in their cottage.'

The pigeons in the eaves ruffled their feathers. The voles in the cupboards shivered.

'I'm not going to hurt you,' said Snow White.

The dwarves sat down to a breakfast of omelettes.

'Delicious! So delicious!' they said as they gobbled up the fresh eggs.

'I'm glad you think so,' said Snow. 'Your lunches await you on the windowsill.' And she pointed to where seven lunch pails stood steaming in the sunshine. The dwarves' eyes widened. They grabbed their pails and sniffed the scents curling from within.

'Mmm,' they said. 'Meat stew.'

Snow smiled.

The dwarves busied themselves stepping into their work boots and pulling on their gloves while Snow washed their breakfast dishes in the sink by the window and watched them from the corner of one eye. She noticed they gathered in a hushed huddle by the front door, and thought she heard a grinding sound like a very old lock being forced, but in seconds the dwarves were bidding her good morning as they stepped out in single file. Axes over their shoulders, they set off for the diamond mines. The cottage fell quiet.

Snow washed her way through the dishes at the kitchen sink, whistling as she worked. Presently she heard a rustling in the undergrowth. She stopped whistling, and reached up to a shelf above the window where she'd stored her bow and arrows out of sight of her little housemates. She wrapped her fingers round them, poised. An old hag emerged through the trees and approached the cottage. Snow White released the weapon.

'Peace be with you, young woman,' said the hag, shuffling up to the window.

'Peace be with you, old woman,' said Snow White.

'I have vegetables for sale. Anything you need, miss?'

Snow wiped her hands on her apron. 'I've seven hungry men to feed this evening. What can you offer me?'

'Seven men? You have your work cut out, young woman. How about potatoes, some carrots and some onions? Find yourself a rabbit and you'll have a fine stew for those hard-working men of yours.'

Snow shook her head. 'I've a good stock of meat myself.' She smiled at the squeal that came from a cupboard by her feet. 'How much might you be asking for the vegetables?' she said.

'For you, miss, as it's your first order there'll be no charge. I'll even throw in some mushrooms as well, how about that?'

Snow smiled and held out her apron through the window. 'I'd say that sounds perfect,' she said. The women smiled at each other as they passed the wares from wrinkled grey hands to smooth white ones.

'I can turn the most basic ingredients into a meal fit for a king,' said Snow.

'You must be well taught, young woman.'

'By the best,' said Snow.

The dwarves arrived home at dusk, glittering with diamond dust from their day's labour. They called out to Snow from their huddle in the doorway.

'We could smell your cooking all the way from Bumbleton Bridge!' they cried. 'There is no greater luxury than having a woman to come home to.'

Snow heard the click of a grinding lock and smiled to herself, then beamed as the dwarves entered the warm kitchen. A fire burned cheerily in the hearth and the scrubbed table was set with seven bowls, seven forks and seven knives. Seven rolls sat on seven napkins beside seven tankards. Snow hauled a cauldron from the fire up onto the table, and the dwarves smacked their lips and rubbed their bellies.

'We're famished,' they said as they scrambled onto chairs and gripped their knives and forks. 'What have you made for us?'

'I made a rabbit and vole stew,' said Snow, ladling the fragrant broth into each bowl. The stew was thick, the meat fell from the bones, the mushrooms were soft and easily speared by the dwarves' forks as they ate and ate.

'Are you not joining us, Miss White?' the dwarves asked as Snow ladled portion after portion into their bowls.

'I already ate,' she said with a smile. 'Besides, what could give a woman greater pleasure than watching a table full of men eat the food she spent all day preparing?'

'But of course! And Miss White, tell us. Did you have any visitors to the cottage today?'

'Not one. Why?'

'Word went around a witch was passing through the

forest today disguised as an old hag selling vegetables. No doubt the vegetables would be enchanted and bring death to whomever were to eat them. You're sure nobody came by trying to sell you anything?'

'If anyone had,' said Snow White, 'I would have heeded what you told me and not answered the door. After all, it's dangerous to open the door to strangers.'

'Of course it is,' said the dwarves. 'You're such a good girl. You're such a good, good—'

The fork of the shortest dwarf clattered to the ground. He clutched at his throat.

'He's choking!' gasped the tallest dwarf, who leapt out of his chair to help, only to stop dead in his tracks, cough, then collapse in spasms on the floor, foaming at the mouth.

Stew splattered to all four corners of the room as bowls were flung aside and tankards knocked asunder as each of the seven dwarves dissolved into spastic choking.

'Poisoned!' they shrieked, pointing trembling fingers up at Snow. 'You witch! You poisoned us!'

They twisted and gagged and writhed on the earthen floor, their eyes rolling back in their heads as they gasped phlegm-choked breaths from closing lungs. In the midst of the pandemonium, Snow White covered her ears with her hands. One by one, each of the seven dwarves shuddered their way into oblivion, eyes bulging, tongues thick, until Snow White stood in the midst of seven purple-faced little corpses. She lowered her palms from her ears. There were no sounds inside the cottage, only whispers from the forest beyond the window: rustling trees, animal feet darting off into unseen distances.

Snow hauled the cauldron off the table, kicked the front door open and strode over to the well. In one smooth motion, she tipped the cauldron over the edge and listened as it clattered against the stones, down, down, getting quieter and quieter, until, finally, there was the faintest of splashes. Snow nodded to herself, then strode back towards the cottage pushing up her sleeves. When she saw who was standing in the doorway, she stopped.

'You were quick,' she said.

'Not as quick as you, my dear,' said the hag. 'Have you got them?'

'No. But I know where they are,' said Snow, closing the front door behind them and dropping to her haunches in front of it. She ran her hands along the rickety wooden floorboards while the hag watched with narrowed eyes, sucking on her one snaggle tooth. Ignoring the splinters, Snow scratched against the grain with her nails, ran her rough palms along the wood and muttered to herself, 'I know it's here.' She pressed, she scratched, she knocked, and then, her nails slipped beneath a gap in the wood so fine she would never have found it had she not seen the dwarves gather in their huddle as they left the cottage.

She prised the floorboard up to see a tiny iron door sealed into the ground with a little sliding iron bar across it. She slid the bar across and heard a lock grind. The door sprang open to reveal a set of keys dusted in glitter. The hag clapped her hands in glee. Snow looked up at her and smiled.

'The diamond mine keys,' she said.

'My wonderful girl,' cried the old hag.

Snow plucked out the keys and got to her feet as the image of the hag shimmered and warped like a reflection in disturbed water, until a woman, tall and as beautiful as a lily, stood before Snow White. The woman placed her hands on the young girl's shoulders.

'You did everything perfectly, my child,' said the Queen.

'Only under your instruction, Mother,' said Snow. 'How is my father, the King?'

'The servants shall find him with his face in his soup.'

'Mushroom?'

'What else?'

The two women laughed and laughed.

'The poisonous ones work quickly,' said the Queen.

Snow jangled the keys. 'And now we have the keys to the only diamond mine in the kingdom.'

'And we, my dear, are about to vanish off the face of the earth,' said the Queen, and waved her hand over Snow White's head.

Snow's vision watered and sounds faded, as though the world around her was falling into memory... When the fog cleared, a black-haired girl of fifteen was no longer standing in front of a crowned, magisterial woman. Two wizened old crones faced each other, beaming toothless grins below their hooked noses, midnight capes draped over their identical humps.

'Do we have to be ugly?' groaned Snow White.

'The best way for women to move unhindered through this world is to be either ugly or old or both. No one will trouble us. We shall mine our diamonds then fly with our loot to our new life, just you and I.'

Despite her outward appearance, Snow found she was not afflicted with the physical ailments of age. She stepped easily over the bodies of the dwarves to retrieve her bow and arrows from the kitchen shelf. When she emerged from the cottage, she saw her mother mounted on her chestnut mare. Snow's own dappled white horse awaited her, prancing and stamping, eager to be off.

Snow White launched up onto her horse, and the two ugliest crones in the land galloped off into the forest, their white hair billowing in the forest breeze.

Home Schooling

By Shannon Savvas

A New Zealand writer who divides her life between New Zealand, England and Cyprus. Shortlisted for The Bridport Prize, Kilmore Literary Festival Write by the Sea, Allingham Festival in 2021. Longlisted for Sligo Cairde Short Story Award, Flash500. Was nominated for the 2020 Pushcart. Won a few, lost more. Made a few shortlists, longlists, and published online, in anthologies and magazines.

Desert Road, New Zealand. November 1985

Caoimhe Connelly was blithely unconcerned that her parents were waking two hundred odd miles north, asking *where the hell has she gone this time?* Jandals kicked off, feet on the dash, she read the DepEd leaflet (Home Schooling Curriculum) while her kids slept in the back of Neil's Pontiac Firebird eating the miles south to Wellington.

'Listen to this, Babe. Key Competencies. Should be fun.

'One – Thinking – yep, that's a good start. Cause and effect thinking involves exploring how actions cause predictable changes... etc, etc.

'Two – Using language/symbols/text. Finding meaning based on personal knowledge, experiences and beliefs.

'Three – Jeez, how many of these are there? Managing self, understanding sometimes there is no one right answer. Making decisions... yada, yada, yada. No right answer, my arse.

'Four – Relating to others, accommodating a diversity of people by listening, seeing different points of view, negotiating and more blah, blah, blah.

'And Numero fivo – Participating/contributing. Challenging children to be ready, willing, and able to step up, take action, and be involved in situations and in life.

'Christ Al-fucking-mighty. Give me a break. All I gotta do is teach them to do what they're told, or there'll be trouble. Keep stuff private. No yakking to nosy neighbours, sneaky grand-parents or police. Get the right change when I send them to buy cigarettes and read lots of library books.'

Caoimhe ripped up the booklet and tossed it out the window. 'Easy-peasy.'

The Bay, Marlborough Sounds. March 1986

Mum ran bare-footed and whooping down the jetty into Neil's arms. He'd been gone since Christmas on a fishing trawler out of Nelson. She danced around, getting in Neil's way as he helped the postie-cum-pilot of the mailboat offload beer and groceries.

'What did you bring me, Babe?'

Jordan roared up on his ATV to collect his supplies. Neil back-slapped his cousin.

'Hey Jordy, you good?'

'Yeah. The kids said you were coming in today. Liesl says come up if you guys want lunch.'

'Yay!' Tildy and I shouted.

'Sounds good, mate.'

'No thanks, Jordan, I've got something hot and delicious waiting for Neil,' Mum said winking.

Jordan blushed. Neil snorted.

Tildy laid the table while Mum reheated the shepherd's pie. When Neil walked in from his shower, nuddy but for a towel wrapped around his waist, she said, 'Christ, hadn't realised how hungry I am.' She hugged Neil close, nuzzled his neck. 'You didn't want Liesl's foreign muck, did you? All that cabbage? I swear I hear their farts down here.'

Tildy banged the plates on the table. 'Anything would be better than mince again.'

After lunch, Neil doled out chocolate. 'Skedaddle. Don't come back until teatime.'

Tildy got the nets and jars, I grabbed the buckets. We had a crab farm to finish building.

'Take the baby with you,' Mum said.

It was dark when we got home. They were zonked out in the bedroom. Mum was buried under her quilt next to Neil who was making pig noises in his sleep, the air thick with the tang of her special baccy and beer. Tildy closed the door and turned on the front room light.

'We've an hour of power. Bathe Stefan and give him his bottle. If you get him to sleep, I'll make hundreds and thousands sammies for tea,' she said gathering the overfull ashtrays and empties littering the floor.

That night, bum-to-bum, heel-to-heel under the duvet on the sofa bed, I wished we were at Gran's in Nelson.

With Neil home, Mum's typewriter fell silent. They drank and smoked and danced the week away. Tildy, me and the baby trawled the beaches, pretending to be princesses banished by their wicked stepmother to the castle-like rocks in the bay where Tildy declared to the sea, 'I will never marry. I will ride a big white horse with my trusted band of friends. I will marry a prince and have lots of babies.' She waved her driftwood sword at me. 'And I will love them all.'

I cheered her on and fed sand pies to Tiger Lily, the doll our real dad had brought me all the way from China. The gold embroidery edging her ruby-red jacket had frayed into long yellow tendrils but I loved her.

One day, bored with the shore, we roamed the upper paddocks. Liesl showed us the new piglets snuggled against their fat mother.

'Are you hungry?' she asked.

We nodded.

'*Komm.* I've made my mummy's *Spaetzle mit Käse.*'

'What's that?' I asked.

'Wait and see, Schatzi.'

In the kitchen, Liesl plonked Stefan on a chair with a big cushion, tied him with a scarf, and let him shovel every noodle nub spread before him into his mouth with little fat fists. Her macaroni cheese tasted better than the canned stuff mum bought. Trixie their old sheepdog hoovered what fell on the floor.

Liesl wrapped apple pastry slabs in greaseproof paper for us to eat later. '*Komm* back any time.'

'She talks funny,' I said as we walked along the beach track.

'She's German.' Tildy's voice dropped to a whisper. 'Mum says they can't make babies.'

'Why not?' I asked.

She shrugged.

We made shell pictures on the mudflats and ate Liesl's apple cake on the jetty while Stefan slept in the shade. Tilda read her new Mallory Towers from the Havelock library, scribbling on a scrap of paper in her pocket with one of Mum's stubby pencils.

'What are you writing?'

'Words I don't know.'

We sat on the warm boards, legs dangling until Mum shouted teatime.

I pushed my plate of Watties' tinned macaroni and cheese away.

'What's up, Eebee?' Mum asked.

'Liesl's was nicer.'

Mum stopped moving. 'How would you know?'

'We had lunch there. And she made bread with walnuts and gave us apple pie for afters,' I said. 'It was gorgeous.'

'Liesl said she'd made too much anyway,' Tildy said.

'Then I guess you're not hungry.' Mum slammed the pot in the sink. 'Bedroom. Now.'

'I don't want to.' I sniffed back the tears.

'Do as you're told, you little shit.'

'Come off it, Keeva. They're kids,' Neil said. 'Liesl was being nice.'

'Nice my arse. Fucking sterile *Hausfrau*.'

In the bedroom, Mum took out her black, brass-buckled belt.

'We are not bloody scroungers.' Thwack! 'Don't you dare go there again.' Thwack! 'You're my kids. Not hers.' Thwack! 'You eat here, got it?'

Thwackthwackthwack...

Next morning, from our sofa bed we watched Neil squinty-eyed behind his cigarette smoke, drinking his morning cuppa.

'Christ. It's not even seven.' Mum leaned against the bedroom door in Neil's rumpled Bowie tee rubbing her face.

'Mum's not wearing pants,' I whispered.

'Shush,' Tildy said.

'What are you two sniggering about?' Mum took a drag on Neil's cigarette.

'Nothing.' We burrowed out of sight.

'I'm giving Jordy a hand to clear the back paddock,' Neil said pulling on his work boots. 'He's putting in a greenhouse for Liesl to grow herbs and veggies.'

'Jesus. You've been working your arse off at sea for months.'

'Gotta show willing. We're not paying rent.'

'It's a crappy bach. Electricity twice a day and I wouldn't put a dog in it. Big fucking deal.'

'Okay Lady Muck, take your kids and shove off.'

'Yeah? And where would I go?'

'Exactly. Quit whining.'

'Maybe it's Liesl's milkmaid tits that've got you going?'

'Yeah, well, they would if I didn't have yours, Babe.'

Two weeks later, Neil left for another fishing trip. A week later, Jordan mentioned taking his boat over to Havelock for tractor parts, did we need anything?

'I'll come with you,' Mum said. 'I'm going stir crazy.'

'What's "stir crazy", Tildy?'

Tildy shrugged and got her notebook.

'You kids coming as well?' Jordy said.

'No, they're not.'

A hundred pleases, a thousand promises got us nowhere.

'No. I can't shop, go to the library, and pick up the benefits trailing you three.'

'They're a bit young to leave alone, I'll tell Liesl to keep an eye out.'

'Don't bother.'

'Be at the jetty by ten, Keeva.'

Tildy waited until he'd gone.

'You don't want anyone to know we're not in school,'

'Oh, you're a snide little bitch.'

Mum and Tildy had a who'll-look-away-first standoff. Tildy won. Mum walked to the bedroom to change. She came out wearing high heels and a floaty dress which showed her boobs.

'For your information Miss Know-it-all, I'm home schooling you, aren't I?'

Tildy snorted. 'You call library books home schooling? We want to go to school.'

'We don't have any friends,' I said. Tildy's boldness catching.

'Tough. Friends are overrated. They always end up shitting on you.'

'If we're such a bother, why can't we live with Grandma and Granddad?' Tildy asked.

'Same problem as friends.'

'You could come and see us when you got... spoon crazy.'

I adored Grandma, with her beads and bangles, fantastical stories and Irish rebel songs.

'Leave you with that mad bitch and her Catholic mumbo jumbo? Over my dead body.' Mum lit a cigarette. 'Anyway, what makes you think they'd want you?'

'Grandma said—'

Mum clipped my head. 'Grandma's full of shit. She'd have Tildy alright. Down the confessional and in the clutches of some paedo-priest putting more than Holy Communion in her mouth. Stefan she'd twist into her own fucked idea of a man. But you, Eebee. Who would want a baby orang-utan at their table? Christ, not even I want you.'

Tildy put her arms around me. 'I want you.'

'Oh, stop blubbing, Eebee.'

'Send us to boarding school if you don't want us around.'

'I wish.'

'Dad would pay,' Tildy said.

'Yeah, right. Besides, boarding school's not like that Blyton shit you read.'

'Anything would be better than this bullshit.' Tildy ran at her, fists ready, wild.

'Cut the dramatics.' Mum shoved her back on top of me next to Stefan on the sofa, crushing us both.

Tildy held Stefan, cooing into his ear. 'You only want us here to look after Stefan. You're just mean. I hate you. I don't care if you're our mother. We hate you.'

'Piss off. Don't expect me to bring you anything back from town.' Mum flounced to the bedroom. Carole King's *Will You Still Love Me Tomorrow* poured under the door.

'Now who's being dramatic,' Tildy said. 'Let's go for a swim.'

Jordan returned alone from Havelock.

'She didn't show, kids. She'll probably catch a ride on tomorrow's mailboat. Stay with us tonight.'

We refused. We both knew Mum would skin us alive if we did.

Liesl walked down, hoping to persuade us but Tildy politely said no again.

'We're not allowed. Besides, we're used to it.'

'I'm sure you are Mathilde.'

Tildy smiled. She loved hearing Liesl's accent make her proper name sing.

'But you shouldn't be.' Liesl squeezed her lips until they turned the colour of pumice. A wobble flicked across her chin. 'Also, we will come to you. *Zu essen.*'

Liesl called it a goulash. Tildy and I called it scrummy. The best bit was her cake bursting with berries. Liesl fed Stefan on her knee, laughing at the mess he made of them both, until tears dribbled on her chin.

'Why are you crying, Liesl?' I asked.

'Ach, *Schnuckiputzi*. I got dust in my eye.'

Tildy hooted. 'Shnooki what?'

'Yordan what's *Schnuckiputzi* in English?'

'Cutie-pie, Eebee. You're a little cutie-pie.'

'Am I?' I blushed. No one had called me cute before.

Tildy asked him how they met.

'She was working in a bar in London and kept giving me extra shots with my beer. Her intentions were definitely not honourable.' His wink brought a small smile to Liesl's face.

'What's "honourable"?' I asked.

'It means she was head over heels in love with me,' Jordan said. 'Couldn't help herself. Well, who could? I'm such a *schnuckiputzi*.' Even Stefan laughed.

Later, she sang a clapping song until Stefan drifted off to sleep. '*Backe, backe Kuchen, der Bäcker hat gerufen,*' she sang quietly.

'Was that German?' Tildy asked.

'Yes. It's about a baker baking cake. Now, little sparrows get ready for bed.'

The next day, Liesl brought tomato soup and herb-flecked dumplings in a tureen decorated with tiny pink and blue flowers with warm walnut bread wrapped in a clean tea towel for lunch.

Tildy pulled an almost clean, crumpled sheet from the laundry basket and laid it on the table.

'Go get some flowers, Eebee,' she whispered.

I returned with pink and blue hydrangeas, just like Liesl's soup pot. Tildy washed the nearly finished honey jar crawling with ants, before putting the flowers in the middle of the table.

Liesl's eyes definitely got all weepy when she saw them, but that's when Mum hullaballooed from the pier. Tildy grabbed Stefan and we ran down to where Mum was waving and whooping on a big black inflatable.

'Who wants pressies?' she shouted.

A bloke with a beard jumped onto the wharf and secured the Zodiac before helping Mum off. He was the spitting image of Captain Haddock.

'Surprise! Lolly scramble!' She tipped up a paper bag onto the jetty.

We dove down, shrieking and stuffing our pockets.

'Gidday mate, Mike Abbot.' He held out his hand to Jordan. 'Didn't mention nippers, Keeva.'

'They won't bother us, Mike.' She turned to Jordan. 'Mike's heading over to Maud Island, he's a researcher for the Conservation Department. He kindly offered to help a lady out, seeing as you left me high and dry, Jordan.'

'I waited an hour for you.' Jordan's fists bunched as he leaned in close to Mum. 'Where the hell were you? You stink of booze.'

Mike stepped between them. 'Mate, I don't...'

Jordan shoved him. 'Piss off. I'm not your mate.'

Mike ripped off his moorings and roared away.

'Liesl's cooked us lunch,' I said. 'There's plenty if you're hungry, Mum.'

Mum charged up to the bach, burst in the door and backed Liesl against the table.

'Get the fuck out of here and away from my children, you fucking German cow.'

'Watch your bloody tongue, Keeva,' Jordan said.

'Just because she's barren as the bloody Gobi Desert doesn't mean she can play mumsy with my kids.'

'Neil's gonna hear about this.'

'Fuck Neil.'

Mum was raging. Wrecked, wasted and raging. She pushed them out the door, hurled Liesl's beautiful dish and bread after them. Hot soup splattered everywhere. Liesl was crying as she picked up the pieces.

That evening, Jordan hammered on the door.

Mum flung it open. 'What?'

'You and your kids leave on next week's mailboat. Otherwise, I'll report you to the police.'

That night, Tildy wrapped around me, singing Liesl's song, making up the words, making them funny until the welts stopped stinging the back of my legs. Tildy drifted off. Mum was snoring. Stefan blew tiny milk breaths. The stinging came back.

Next morning, Mum made scrambly eggs, muttering bitch-*kraut* between ciggie sucks. 'Eat up, then disappear. Mike's bringing me some good shit. Tildy, make sandwiches for lunch. And you, you little bitch, stop snivelling,' she said pointing at me. 'Keep Stefan quiet and don't go near that

Nazi up at the farm.'

Captain Haddock turned up at the jetty in his noisy boat where we were fishing. He asked where our place was.

'Why?' Tildy said.

'I've... ah... brought your mum a present.'

'Wacky-baccy?' He nodded. Tildy waved him on. 'That way.'

Stefan, who'd been pulling at his ear all morning, began crying, his cheeks red and hot and scratchy under my fingers. We pulled up the lines and walked to our usual beach. Once in the water, he stopped crying. Later under the trees, he fell asleep on a bed of towels.

'Can we have a picnic, Tildy?'

'You betcha. Marmite and lettuce or lettuce and marmite sammies for lunch?'

'Well now Tildy, I think marmite and lettuce. Definitely.' We fell about laughing.

She gave me a hug. 'Watch Stefan. I'll see if there's any squashed-fly bikkies as well. I won't be long.'

Stefan woke crying before she got back. I picked him up, put him down, sang *Incy Wincy Spider*, *The Wheels on the Bus*, Liesl's clapping song. Still, he cried. Heavy and hot, his nappy full of smelly, runny poo, he squirmed when I tried to hug him, bumped his head on my teeth and screamed. There was no sign of Tildy, so I stripped off his stripy onesie and shorts, bundling his yucky nappy in Tildy's bucket. I plonked him in the shallow waters of the returning tide and let them wash over his fat legs and bum while I swished his clothes and laid them to dry on the rocks. He was happy splish-splashing, so I grabbed my yellow bucket and scrambled over the rocks to check our crab farm before the tide came right in.

The old fruit box covered in chicken wire we'd wedged between the rocks to catch the tide-born crabs was empty.

Its slats were gummy and black after a couple of weeks washed by the waters, the wire curled back. The tide was running but still a way out so I clambered over to the best rock pools. I managed to catch a few big-handed crabs, a couple of hermits and one swifty before the rocks were swallowed by the incoming sea. They'd have to do. I was hungry and Tildy should be back with lunch.

Back at our camp, marmite and lettuce sandwiches spilled across the sand. Further out, Tildy was mucking about in the water.

'Tildy! Whatcha doing?'

'Get Mum, or Jordan. Anybody. And don't come back. Quick, Eebee!'

I ran and ran. Mum and Mike wouldn't wake up until I screamed.

'Mum! Stefan's dead. It's my fault. Tildy's trying to...'

After the police and rescue helicopter arrived, after the howling, after the shouting, Mum cried all night.

Tildy got her wish and went to Grandma's in Nelson.

Mum kept me home.

The lessons she taught me were not in the Department of Education's home-schooling curriculum.

Believe Me

By Victoria Dence

Victoria Dence is a 20 year old English student at Bournemouth university. She became interested in creative writing from a young age after being an avid reader throughout school. Upon choosing English as a degree, Victoria specifically chose units which included creative writing assignments. Whilst continuing to write in her spare time she has also chosen a creative dissertation and will be writing poetry within this later on in the year.

The night ended just as it had begun: a figure slumped in a dimly lit flat with only the low hum of the television breaking the silence.

I started my day in the same manner I did every other, waking up ten minutes before the alarm with that same heavy feeling in the pit of my stomach, sitting in bed willing the night to return, and eventually dragging myself up to make a cup of tea.

My small one-bedroom flat was my sanctuary, from the brightly coloured rugs and throws, to the unnecessary number of plants I obsessed over. My favourite place had to be my mezzanine floor; a platform situated halfway up the wall, perfectly aligning with the morning sunlight shining in through the window on the opposite side. On this half-floor was where I slept, it felt comforting being closer to the ceiling, less empty space for my imagination to fill in with menacing shadows. I had always struggled with my overactive imagination or, as the doctor called it, 'Generalised Anxiety Disorder'. In my mind, it meant I was prepared to face any danger, always on guard, but what this also meant was that I spent an unwarranted amount of time planning every tiny detail of my life. It had now got to the point where I found it difficult to leave the flat.

My phone buzzed, yet another sound that instilled dread in me. Three messages popped up from the 'girls' group chat; 'Drinks at yours tonight, Lilah??' one of them read. These girls were my closest friends, but I still couldn't help but feel nervous ahead of our plans.

I spent the rest of the day rushing around the flat pushing around my clutter in an attempt to make it look presentable. The evening was my favourite part of the day; I could turn on all my string lights and lamps and make the flat cosy. I felt safe blocking out the world. Nestling into my favourite chair, I watched the clock. The doorbell rang, and

I rushed to let them in. Shannon, Lucy, and Liv bustled in giggling, clearly already a bit tipsy.

'We've found the cheapest vodka. Look at this, Lilah,' Shannon slurred, holding up the clear bottle with a third missing from the top.

'Pour me a shot?' I asked. I needed to catch up if I didn't want to become the designated babysitter. The flat came alive whenever I had friends round: the animated chatter, the clinking of glasses, and the gentle beat of background music. The few drinks I'd had dulled the gentle uneasiness in my body, that constant reminder that I was never fully relaxed.

As the evening drew to a close, a sleepy atmosphere settled over the flat, the twinkling lights blurred into a warm glow encapsulating our small circle. The conversation had moved onto discussions of dreams and how in love Lucy was with a guy she had met once. I leaned over and switched on the TV, a gentle hint that the evening was ending, and my bed was calling.

Out of the corner of my eye, I spotted a shadow move swiftly past the frosted window in my front door. My heart felt as though it had dropped out of my chest and my posture switched from relaxed to bolt upright. I slowly got up in an attempt to remain casual in front of my friends. At this point my breathing was speeding up and becoming a conscious effort. I heard a man's voice out in the hallway. The familiar panic was setting in; my whole body was sent into survival mode. Without a second thought I ran into the kitchen grabbing the nearest knife. All I knew was that I was in danger; there was a man and he wanted to hurt me. I hurtled past my friends and pushed myself out of the front door. My sweaty palms gripped onto the cool metal of the knife, and I stumbled forwards brandishing it at the man. I felt hands grab my waist and I was pulled backwards.

'What the fuck are you doing, Lilah?' Liv had grabbed me and was screaming questions at me. 'What is wrong with you? You could have hurt him.' I switched my gaze upwards and spotted my elderly neighbour, Jim, a few feet away clutching a shopping bag.

'I was just popping back from the Co-op,' his voice trembled as he spoke.

'It's alright, Jim,' Shannon spoke more gently now, 'she's just had a bit too much to drink. You get home, okay?'

He nodded and shuffled into his flat. I slumped down into a crouching position, tears filling my eyes, my heart still pounding

'I'm so sorry, I thought he was an intruder I didn't me–' I spoke in between sobs staring up at three concerned faces.

After a while, we stumbled back into the entrance of the flat.

'We're worried about you, Lilah. You can't keep acting like this,' Liv said. They had seen a few of my anxiety attacks but never one as bad as this. I felt as if I wasn't in control of my own body, I didn't know myself anymore. After about fifteen minutes of awkward chatter and an abundance of worrying glances between my friends, they finally got ready to leave.

'Are you going to be alright?' Lucy asked in a soft voice.

'Yep, I'll be fine.' I was tired of talking about my problems. I just wanted to curl up in the safety of my bed.

Once they had all left, I switched off a few of the lights but kept the television on at a low volume; the soft atmosphere released some of my tension. I climbed up the sturdy wooden ladder which led to my mezzanine floor. Too tired to get undressed, I got into bed and pulled the covers tightly up to my chin. The events of the evening meant it was even more difficult for me to relax. I stared blankly at the ceiling tracing the outline of the shadows my plants had cast up through the dim lighting.

I woke abruptly to a high-pitch grating noise coming from my window. My body tensed and my eyes widened adjusting to the dimly lit flat. I fumbled around for my phone under a tangle of blankets. Upon finding it I switched it on, the bright screen straining my eyes. The time read 23:07. I shakily peered down past the ladder, my eyes searching for the source of the sound. The scraping sound came again, this time coming from the front door. I began to panic but tried to remain rational, remembering what happened earlier that evening. I clutched my phone, trembling as I typed in my password and opened up contacts, scrolling frantically searching for someone who would answer this late. I pressed 'Call' on Lucy's contact willing her to pick up. The dialling tone stopped, and I heard a bleary voice come out from the phone. 'Hello?' whispered Lucy.

'Lucy, I'm panicking. There's a sound coming from my door. I think someone is trying to get in.' My words tumbled out in between short breaths.

'OK. Think about this logically, Lilah. You've already made up one event tonight. It'll just be the wind.' Her voice sounded weary; I knew I had put them through a lot, but this was the time I really needed her.

'Please, I don't know what to do anymore! I don't want to feel like this, but perhaps you're right. I'll try to calm myself.' I chose to lie; it was better to keep her as a friend than to keep pushing her away even further.

'Alright, Lilah. Just try and get some sleep now; you know we all love you. We just want what's best.'

'Thank you, Lucy.' I had nothing left to say. I knew she thought I was making it all up. I sat rigidly, my legs pulled up to my body and my back pressing into the wall. I remained in this position for a while, my ears straining and searching for that terrifying sound again. My breathing was calming down a bit now. Maybe my friends were right; I didn't want to scare anyone with my rash decisions.

The absence of the sound should've been a small comfort but all I could think was how threatening it seemed. Did that mean someone was inside watching me? I *had* to start fighting my fears. I couldn't live as this quivering mess my whole life.

Still clutching onto my phone, my lifeline, I clambered down the ladder, looking around me at each step I took. Seeing the remnants of our evening made me relax a little; a scatter of used bottles and glasses littered the table, abandoned snacks were a gentle reminder that I was in the real world.

I whipped my head around spotting a dark shadow through the frosted window. Almost instantly it had disappeared. I was struggling to keep in touch with reality. The security light flashed on in the hallway and I heard a loud thud followed by silence then darkness. I closed my hands into tight fists, feeling the sweat forming, the blood rushing through my ears in a pounding rhythm. I inched closer to the door, my eyes remaining glued to the window. I reached out towards the door handle, my arm feeling detached from the rest of my body. The metal felt cool against my hot, sweating hands. I gripped the handle and pushed down. The door creaked open slightly. Through the gap, I saw a figure lying twisted on the concrete floor. My eyes scanned up the body towards the face, his elderly appearance instantly familiar. I shook as I took a further step towards the pale body of my neighbour, Jim. In my panic, I grabbed his face trying to wake him up.

'Jim, please wake up,' I sobbed.

His neck was stiff and his eyes remained wide open. I

didn't want to believe it was too late. Travelling down his body, I pushed hard on his chest with two hands. I could barely see through the tears falling down my face, dripping onto him. As I tried to pump life back into him, I noticed a wet sticky feeling on my hands. Lifting them up, I gazed down at the dark red blood covering my hands and his shirt. At this point I was struggling to breathe; I knew he was gone. I sat back on my knees, defeated. For what felt like hours I sat there, staring down at my hands, my whole body shaking uncontrollably.

Eventually, I remembered the phone in my pocket. I reached for it, covering the phone in blood, and slowly dialled 999. I didn't want Jim lying out on the cold floor; he deserved to be in a safe place. After all, it was me who couldn't save him. I grabbed on to his shoulders and began dragging him into my flat. With the adrenaline still coursing through my veins, I managed to haul him up onto my sofa. His body slumped into an unnatural position; my once cosy flat now looked like a crime scene.

Hours later I sat in the police station, my head scrambled from the events of this evening. I had given them the names of my friends to account for my whereabouts at the time and told them how I had heard an intruder moments before Jim died. An officer came and sat next to me. She could see I was struggling but spoke firmly.

'From what your friends have told us, you had already attempted to attack the deceased gentlemen earlier tonight. We have found traces of your DNA all over him, and, after a search of your flat, a knife matching the one used was found. As a result, we will be arresting you on suspicion of his murder.' She placed handcuffs on my wrists. They clamped shut before I could even say another word.

The Cabbage Killer

By Fred Cummings

Fred lives in the Purbecks. He credits his rural youth, and a career spent on the building sites of darkest Dorset, as the source of his interest in the portrayal of human motivation and character.His writing could be considered social realism, which he hopes expresses the humour and pathos of the human condition.

'Sit up to the table boy,' he snarled.

'Listen to your father, George,' Mother yelled from the kitchen.

George spent the periods of waiting below the table, parading his soldiers across the worn expanse of carpet. Father sat at his end of the table with his radio at his elbow. The large set was covered in dials and knobs, and George imagined his father eagerly awaiting some crackling transmission from a distant land. Father was listening eagerly, but to the Radio Four news, and he growled out his disapproval accordingly.

George was wary of the smell from the kitchen. Father's damp woollen socks recently aired from their wellington boots was a preferable smell. The steaming food George suffered was always from the garden, which sounds comforting, but by a reasoned comparison, Father's food appeared oversized, bland and fibrous. A great quantity of vegetable matter heaped on a plate. Dinner time was a trial and tonight George knew by the sweet earthy smell he was doomed. The newsreader's voice boomed with some urgency as George took his place, a diminutive referee between the combative ends of the table. Father did not delay and pounced on his food. His nostrils flared in the steam.

Father's generation wasted no food. Fat, trotter, cheek, rind and bone were valued. Meat was won at the pub or shared between friends. George though, felt boiled ox tongue on a bed of cabbage was surely a cruelty too far. A livery waft of the tongue made him fidget in his chair.

'Just try it can't you, George?' Mother pleaded. George felt his throat closing, tears brimming his lower lids. His hand crept past the plate towards the salt. Down struck the flattened knife blade onto his fingers.

'You don't need salt, damn you!' Strong words followed

between Mother and Father, but George's senses had shut down. Eventually the radio stopped, and he was alone at the table, Father reclining in the lounge and Mother washing up.

'George, put these peelings on the compost heap would you please.'

'And stay away from the cabbage rows!' Father shouted after him.

It was true. George had been guilty of crawling, commando style, through the cabbages, the great leathery leaves hiding his progress. Father found a soldier abseiling down a pea string once. George accepted the casualties of war. He knew the soldier would be thrown into the privet hedge behind the potting shed.

A narrow strip of turf ran centrally down the length of the garden to the distant compost heap. Bathed in the setting sun, the cabbages on either side seemed exotic and George rallied as he strode giant-like through the stunted jungle. Emptying the bucket, he looked back at his mother's illuminated face over the kitchen sink. She was crying. Even at the extremity of the long garden, it was obvious.

George adopted his commando crawl. It was not helpful for Mother to know he'd seen her crying. Laying prone on the cool grass, George accepted he must do something. Though this would be no reckless bayonet charge at the back door, he told himself. Then the idea struck him like a stun grenade. He inched his way into the cabbage rows and, with a bamboo cane, probed the loose soil at the base of the nearest cabbage. The cane found the thick taproot. George destroyed the hair-like roots that surrounded it. He levelled the soil surface. It appeared undisturbed, but for the cabbage the war was over. He made his way back to the house through the minefield of cabbages, stirring the roots randomly.

George slept well, waking to a dry bed for once. Mother smiled her approval.

'He'll be late for work if he stands around staring at those cabbages all morning,' she said, drawing the curtains wide. George sprang from the bed to the window, his hands on the sill like a dog at a table. His father's head was bowed, gazing from one plant to another. The leaves had wilted, hanging limp on the stalk. It was then that George knew: he'd turned cabbage killer.

At dinner time that evening Father appeared distracted, and George knew the reason why. By Sunday morning things had turned critical. Father consulted every almanac and gardening textbook he could. On tenterhooks, he listened to *Gardener's Question Time*, to hear of some plague or pestilence cast over the land. Percy Thrower revealed nothing. The man who brought the ox tongue turned up but could offer no help. They stood together poking the rotting stalks with the bamboo cane. Every caterpillar and grub was a suspect, every worm or maggot a culprit. But soon only the slugs seemed interested in the blackened slime that was once the plump cabbage leaves. Father harvested the remaining healthy cabbage, Mother freezing what she could.

George saw the impending shortage; soon it was apparent. One evening they had baked beans at dinner, another time rice with sweetcorn. Things got so good George thought *The Tiger Who Came to Tea* might turn up. The garden was empty, the soil bare. But soon little green sproutings appeared in their neatly spaced rows. It was easy now for George though; one judicious poke and the juvenile plant perished.

Life has certain inevitabilities that George was unaware of. Death, for instance, or the fact that luck eventually runs out. One autumnal Sunday morning when all Winterborne

Clenston should have been asleep, George crept to the cabbage patch. With his back to the house and the sun emerging over the grassy slopes of Netherbury Hill, he performed his destructive ritual. His downfall came when a neighbour spotted him as they drew back their curtains. Later that afternoon Father stood at the front door watching the neighbour gesticulate with an imagined bamboo cane.

George was in the garden when his father came for him. George was quick though and sped down the strip of grass to the boundary that separated the garden from the village playing fields. Father chased hard, though he could not vault the fence as George had. George covered the cricket pitch without looking back and didn't stop till he was halfway up the slope of Netherbury Hill. From his vantage point he watched his father abandon the chase and walk back across the cricket pitch, their tracks glistening in the evening dew.

Soon Father was in the cabbage patch wiping his brow with his large white handkerchief. George had no wish to move or any idea what to do for that matter, so he sat in the long grass and watched. Father stooped over the seedlings, forking the earth. Suddenly Father stood bolt upright, dropping the garden fork. George thought Father had been shot. Father's face screwed up in pain. His hands clasped his chest as he fell backwards into the dirt. George sat frozen and uncomprehending. Mother ran down the strip of grass to the cabbage patch.

The church bell pealed for the start of evensong as George saw the ambulance rushing through Long Clenston. Father was taken away under a white sheet. George waited till Mother turned the house lights on before coming home.

For some time, George enjoyed playing in the scrubby overgrowth that had once been the cabbage patch. One day Uncle Albert, Mother's brother, turfed the lot over and planted a crab-apple tree where Father fell. George let the tree live, collecting the windfalls for Mother. He returned to his spot on Netherbury Hill many times. Even in his adulthood, he returned to see how the crab-apple tree had grown. Occasionally George wondered how things would have been if he had stopped halfway across that cricket pitch. Different perhaps, perhaps not; but he felt sure he would still have an abiding hatred of both Radio Four and cabbages.

Her Spectres

by Bhagath Subramanian

Bhagath Subramanian is a writer and artist currently based in Bournemouth. Their work is primarily influenced by world cinema and photography. They enjoy telling stories through a variety of mediums, such as film and interactive narratives. Otherwise, they're a simple living thing that spends their time doing living thing stuff.

Lucille

They seemed strong. Or was it cold? The father was steadfast, and the son was unflinching. Everyone expected the mother to be in tears. She always seemed like the type. But her eyes would not water, and her cheeks remained undampened. They sat at the front of the congregation, at the second pew from the altar. They were closer to the wall than the aisle. Everybody expected the mother to be seated nearest to the coffin, closer to the daughter she had loved so dearly.

It was an ordinary funeral, as ordinary as they come. The few that came were dressed in black. A neighbour sobbed quietly. A schoolteacher sat at the back. A police officer was there too. A few friends from the playground were there with their mothers, who weren't sure if a closed casket ceremony was a better or worse thing for a first funeral. Regardless, it is what it is. A little girl had died a most gruesome death. The mother did not cry. No one from the family delivered a eulogy. The schoolteacher did, however. The priest, in a hushed tone, later told one of the other children that different people grieve in different ways.

There were no other relatives present at the funeral. No uncles, no aunts. No grandparents. The family had always been private, distant even. There weren't many who knew of them, and fewer still that actually knew them. The mother used to work late at the library. The father owned a laundromat and kept to himself mostly. The son was hardly ever seen and had moved away the first chance he got. He rolled back into town after he heard of a possible divorce between his parents. The girl had died in a freak car accident a month after that.

The family stayed quiet as they lowered the coffin into the ground. And they were quieter still as they got into their car and drove away, saying very little to all those that had come to see them. There was no reception. Everybody was sure that the three of them had dealt with enough today.

'Stefan', 'Maria', and 'Lars'

Driving was still very new to the father. He was used to simpler systems, automatic ones. He preferred simple machines, ones with very few parts. This car was unwieldy to him. It was something that he would have to put time into. Maybe next week.

As they rolled into the driveway, they noticed that the front door was open. They had forgotten to close it when they left this morning. It brought them no concern. They lived far from anyone else and were surrounded by thick forest. A wandering animal in the kitchen would be no problem, and a person wouldn't have entered at all. They got out the car, leaving the engine running. On the way inside, the mother left the door open, forgetting to shut it. She took off her boots and her jacket, then turned to go into the kitchen. On the stove was the cast iron pan she had used to prepare breakfast. The hob was still turned on, and the flame was on high. She slowly walked over to the stove and turned the gas off. She then grabbed the ripping hot pan with her left hand, not by the handle, but by its edge. She picked it up, and her flesh began crackling and sizzling from the hot metal. She slowly walked over to the sink and turned on the tap. She put the hot pan underneath the water, and then left, leaving the water running.

As she began to make her way to the living room, she raised her left hand to look at it – it was seared, melted in places. The skin had crackled and bubbled up all over, and the fingers were bleeding. She sat on the couch, watching it. She watched until the bubbles began to recede, and the cracks began to stitch back together. Little webs of skin began to crisscross over each other, sealing up the wound.

The fingers began to coat themselves in new patches of skin, coiling up over where the flesh had burst. She watched this unfold over the course of the next two hours. By the end, her left hand had returned to mirroring the right.

The Vehicle

It wasn't like the primitive starships the humans used, clumsy and dangerous, belching out explosion after explosion that propelled them out of the atmosphere, violent and inelegant. Instead, their people used sails, and drifted from star to star on solar winds, sometimes gently catapulting themselves forward by catching the gravity of some moon or a passing asteroid.

The sails were folded away now, and the ship sat in the garage, taking up the same amount of space that the car they left out in the driveway would have. In this dormant state, it was like a fat rose that hadn't unfurled its petals yet. It was a dark grey, and to the human eye it looked as if it was made of rough granite, smoothed down into those ethereal shapes.

'Stefan' decided to let it be for now. They hadn't come into too much danger, and the one unfortunate incident that had happened had been dealt with swiftly (albeit inelegantly, which upset him). There was no point in waking the ship up just to relay that back. He'd include it in his report a few years from now. Anything else would be inefficient.

He began to hear music, from some deeper part of the house. He stepped back inside and recognised the sounds of the vinyl they had interrupted the day they arrived. He elected to walk to the source – better to acclimatise to this form as soon as possible. He felt the microscopic vibrato of the wooden floor through the calcium bones, the fine hairs of his chest brushing against the fabric of his garment, all these sensations gently flicking his nerve endings. It was incredibly tactile, and manual, he thought. He found it all so very humbling. An entire being held together by twine.

'Lars' was already in the living room by the time 'Stefan' entered. 'Maria' was also there, curled up on the sofa, staring at her hand. 'Lars' was looming over the record player. He had no idea what this music was. He wasn't even sure if he enjoyed it. It simply seemed fitting to complete what was interrupted. The words 'CHUCK JACKSON' were printed onto the vinyl's sticker, in a faded maroon colour. He watched the record go round, intrigued by how it wobbled. He decided to poke one side and was both alarmed and charmed by how it screeched in response. He let go. He thought of how fragile it was.

'Stefan' watched the record player from a distance. After the screeching, he went over to the sofa, and decided to sit down next to 'Maria'. There wasn't much to do now but wait, and maybe soak it all in.

Stefan, Maria, and Lars

They had always held elegance and efficiency in the highest regard. Their machines rarely had any moving parts, or made any noise. They did not have computers- they'd long since evolved past the need for artificial intelligence or digital technology.

They preferred silent lives, far from their homeworld. They're known to sail from star to star, looking for a quiet corner in some quieter world. It's what brought them here.

Stefan and Maria had fallen asleep in each other's arms the night they arrived. They'd ploughed through the bottle of wine they were saving, and were listening to the songs they shared with each other when they first met.

Their oldest son, Lars, was in his room. He was home for the Christmas break. He was passed out in bed, the result of his having smoked too much weed during his evening walk and the subsequent overfilling of his belly with apple pie.

Lucille, however, was awake. She liked to sneak into her father's study on nights like this. She'd spend her time carefully pulling books off the shelf and staring at the pictures. And that's where she was when the assimilation began.

Nobody was disturbed when the ship landed. It was an elegant and silent vehicle.

The visitors began with Lars. Quietly, he was broken down into his simplest building blocks. Flesh and bone were slowly lulled into rays of light. His limbs and skull split open, and curled upwards and away from his core, like the strings of a harp snapping underwater. Slowly, they fissured into a glow that engulfed the entire room. He felt no pain.

Where there was once a young man, now stood the beginnings of a new star, in foetal form. Energy and light.

One of them entered the glow.

And in an instant, the glow collapsed in on itself.

There, stood the body of the young man, tipped out and emptied. The first of them claimed this vessel.

'Lars' accompanied the others as they made their way into the living room. They went back down the staircase. The other two glided down without a sound. 'Lars', bound by flesh for the first time, hit the squeaky floorboard.

They did the same to Stefan and Maria.

As they stepped into their new forms, they noticed the girl watching them from the foot of the stairs.

'Maria' reached out and opened her mouth to say something. A guttural groan was all that escaped.

They were too slow and too unused to their unwieldy new bodies to stop her from running out the front door. 'Maria' staggered outside, dragging one foot after the other, growling and wailing. All she could do was watch in confusion as Lucille ran into the street, not seeing the oncoming truck barrelling through the dark winter mist.

Lucille's body was ripped to shreds. A fragile and inelegant little thing. A little creature that might as well have been made of clay.

Home

The three of them hadn't spoken to each other since the assimilation. They hadn't done much at all, apart from eating the occasional thing from the pantry and going to the funeral. They spent their time exploring these new sensations that their new forms provided them, touching various fabrics, running their hands under the sink, and pressing their faces into the cold windows at night.

As 'Stefan' listened to the record play, he decided to reach his hand out to 'Maria'. He placed his palm against the side of her head. He touched her new form for the first time. He felt her warmth. He felt the blood rushing underneath her skin. He felt the tiny hairs that covered her face.

He watched her. And he felt.

'Maria' reached out as well, with her newly sewn together palm. She felt him too.

'Lars' continued to watch the record go round.

Through forms and through space, they were back at the beginning – together, sharing sensation.

Up

By Neil Tully

Neil is a writer from the west of Ireland. He was the overall winner at the Write by the Sea Literary Festival 2021 and was named New Roscommon Writer of the Year 2021. His work has appeared in the Irish Independent, The Honest Ulsterman and elsewhere. He can be contacted at neiltully11@ gmail.com

Opening day at Cheltenham and I'm staring through the wall of screens at Ladbrokes, down two hundred quid. Thinking of ways to make some cash so I don't have to limp back to Mags Forde like a kicked dog, with her crooked teeth and thin lips and fingers in every criminal act in the county. Thinking hard, coming up with nothing.

They've a fan on, blowing failed slips across the dirty carpet, each one a receipt for hope bought with cash, no refunds. There's been ferocious heat all day. First time I've ever seen the regulars use the water cooler. The smell of sweat is powerful. Working man's sweat, drinking man's sweat, gambling man's sweat. Old Gandalf is propped up on a stool, deep breathing gum disease, looking like he's been waterboarded. The commentary from Turffontein is on low, like some anxiety-riddled narration of life in here.

Sully is watching the dogs. He was up twenty-seven quid, so puts a nice round two-euro coin down on trap 4, announcing that it was his final bet of the day. When he walks into Ladbrokes, his wallet tightens like a clenched fist. Smart I suppose. When you're up against it with the bookie, you're either the hare or the greyhound. The hare, Sully, runs for his life, because he's got something worth running for. The greyhound, that's me, does the only thing he knows, and chases even harder. The problem is that today's two hundred wasn't just the dole, but the last of the three thousand, four hundred and twenty-seven euro, sixty-three cents, that Mam left behind in this world. The only thing that was keeping me from Mags' door.

I go and stand next to him, a foot bigger up and across, looking like his bodyguard. The longshot trap 4 dog powers home at 9/1 and Sully's eyes light up at the prospect of a wrinkled twenty coming back across the counter. It's Fat Ray working today. He has a back you could play handball off. Pays out any measly winnings as if it's coming from his own pocket. Good for Sully. But could he not have thrown on twenty? We'd be off to Longnecks with a hundred and eighty quid, having a few pints and laughs and I could forget about Mags for one more cider-soaked evening. I could go home drunk enough to fall asleep, without being tortured by Mam's things. Slippers, hair curlers, hand creams. The plastic basket of medicines, bandages and antiseptics. The bottle of years old perfume she'd *treated* herself to and dabbed on as if it was Christ's tears, still saving it long after it was past its best, our little corner of the world never giving an occasion worthy of its use.

Sully goes to collect and Gandalf leaves with a hacking cough by way of goodbye. Hadn't had a winner all day, same as myself. Think he lives out the straight road, but not sure. See him in here plenty, stroking his beard and never winning, like some unwise mystic.

'Sully, can you spot me twenty? I'll get you back Friday.'

'Course, Mellott,' Sully says. He's only tight with the bookie. If either of us gets a win over 500 quid, we split it, then drink most in celebration. He hadn't even time to pocket his wallet. Opens it up, few notes colour coded, Tesco Clubcard, imprint of a condom coming through from the back compartment. Been in there so long it's as likely to stop a pregnancy as a free bar at a debs. He hands twenty over and doesn't expect thanks, just follows me outside for a smoke.

'Bad luck today,' he says. No further comment needed, so we squint at the Mayo sky then across the car park. Still a heavy heat, the Moy across the road sounding cool and tempting. We nod at a couple of fellas who drive by, on their way home after another day of digging roads, breathing tar, collecting bins, filling skips and lifting blocks with crippled knees. All those jobs given to men without degrees. Home to a three-bed semi, kids screaming about bath time. Wife complaining about their snoring when they finally do drift away from it all. Knackered greyhounds. Chased down the hare they were told to, only when they sank their teeth in, they discovered that it was never real. Like the one at the track. While unseen men made the real money, and now all they can do is keep running in circles.

Sully won't stay around much longer. He's too smart. His family's too good. Went to Galway and got a degree. He's back working with his auld fella, saving for his escape. Dublin first I'd say. Then London, then Zurich or Frankfurt or some European hub where he'll wear suits and watches and meet some leggy, tri-lingual Swiss blonde who'll whip any last bit of Mayo out of him, and he'll get home for a few days at Christmas, then only every other year, and eventually his folks will die and he'll forget this county and this town and these people and these days and this warm March evening when every cent to my name came from his pocket.

I'd have gone to college with him if I could. Got the points I needed. Just never had the money and was looking after Mam while she was on her way out. That's what I told myself anyway. That I was tethered to the place by the collar and a cage. That the Creggs Road son of some feral stray who'd wronged my mother once, doesn't have a way out, isn't bred for colleges or cities or any world beyond this. Never had a reason to think any other way.

'There's one more race if you fancy a last punt? Might come good,' Sully says, his pity as bad as him knowing that the twenty he lent me is all I've left. 'I've been tipping Mr Yeats in the 6.15 all day. Gorgeous bay gelding, priced at 50/1. Saw him run 5th a few weeks back and know he has more in the tank.'

'Yearah I'll leave it Sully. Better strike away home.'

I walk off, round the corner, not sure why I'm pissed

at him. Not pissed at him. Pissed at everything. Pissed to be headed back to Mags, who picked me from a litter of drinkers in McCrann's one night three years back. Nineteen years old, Sully away at college, Mam not able to sit or lie down without agony because of pressure sores on the back of her thighs. Festering, putrid openings with their hateful stink, that I rinsed with saltwater and bandaged and prayed to fuck every morning would look better. I thought maybe Mags knew something of me, was throwing me some work to help out. But she just saw a six-foot-three lad with no job, fists like mallets and nothing to lose. Another dog for her pack.

I put 10 euros of petrol in a canister at Maxol. Enough to get the Intruder back to town when I've cash to fill the tank. I walk the high street, taking the long route, as if a way out will land in front of me before I get to her. Shopkeepers pulling down shutters, Frank the butcher sweeping sudsy water out his door, stink of raw meat coming with it. Oil heating up in the chippie, woman in the Chinese taking phone orders for dinners. Happy hour in Longnecks, the doors open and music coming out.

She put me to work in a dirty bungalow on the edge of town, six 'til two in the morning. Showing my big bulky frame in the hallway and snarling at whatever porn addict came in to use the women that were working the rooms. Usually four on rotation, two on days, two on nights. Eastern European mostly. Once the punter had seen me, I'd go to the back room, making myself scarce in what Mags called her office. Put the takings in a locked top drawer, wrote down the amount each woman had earned in a notepad. Stared at an ashtray overflowing with fag butts for hours on end, while bedposts rattled and fellas came and went, avoiding my eye.

I'd convinced myself for a while that I was just a bouncer.

Eventually realised my job wasn't to keep the women safe. It was to keep them in. Keep them profitable. They were captured prey, laid out for all manner of Mayo's dirty dogs, cute foxes and vicious mink. One night I got home and Mam was dead. I'd left her that evening, vomiting, thinking it was the chicken I'd cooked for her lunch. The pressure sores had gone septic, torn through her skin and poisoned her blood. While I was sitting at Mags Forde's desk, counting her money, helping her to trade in the flesh of other women.

Now I'm going back, out the Racecourse Road, tail between my legs, after swearing I never would. Ten quid and a can of petrol, my lot in life. Stink rising from the can. I wonder can it self-combust in this heat? Send me up in flames by the roadside and maybe I'd be better off. Mags' bungalow is in sight. Makes my stomach lurch. Her van isn't in the yard, but that doesn't mean she's not in. She has skinny Pat Dwyer driving her sometimes, like she's some visiting ambassador.

The gate is open. I walk the long flank of the bungalow, ugly pebble dash, rusted satellite dish, curtains drawn. From the outside, every inch a pensioner's home in need of TLC. I get to the back door and it's all too familiar. Six months since I was here. Give a loud knock and listen for any noise inside. Nothing. A car passes on the road. I knock again, louder. Longer. Heels softened on the lino inside, the blurry shape of a woman through frosted glass.

The door opens. She's late thirties, tired. Brunette. Pink lipstick, some eyeshadow, nothing else on bad skin except a fresh roll of deodorant. She's wearing a dressing gown. Cheap lingerie underneath no doubt. As if a Guard wouldn't spot the six-inch heels.

'Can I help?' she says. No prizes for guessing the accent.

'Mags in?'

'I don't know who you mean,' she says. Well-practised. Scared stiff. You haven't seen violence until you've seen Mags 'teach her girls a lesson'.

I walk in and she shouts something but stands aside all the same, wary and weary of men my size. No muscle appears. The sparse living room's as grim as I remember. Somebody's added a rickety trolley with cheap bottles of spirits from Aldi. Some fairy lights above the window. Has the same rejuvenating effect as giving Lemsip to a man wracked with bowel cancer.

A younger woman comes into the room, black bra and a thong, legs as skinny as a deer's. Eighteen at a push. She says something foreign to the woman behind me who's telling me to get out. I see their eyes meet. Eyes so similar, like mine and my mother's, and I turn to the older woman, thinking of the length Mam would have gone to keep me from Mags' reach, let alone serve me up between her jaws.

'Jesus Christ,' I say. 'Is this your daughter?' I point at the young one and the mother stamps past in her heels, headed for the phone in the office. I follow her in and knock it off the desk, knowing Mags makes them lock up their phones while on duty. I put the can on the desk, and it's either the fumes or the shame or the memories or the thought of the young one in one of those rooms, but my head is spinning. A band of pain working my forehead, jaws pulsing.

'Relax,' I tell her. 'Bloody relax.' I need a second to think. Rubbing my temples, tugging at the neck of my T-shirt. Feeling like the collar is being yanked and the cage is getting smaller.

Sweat pouring off me, heart going like a jockey's whip. I sit at the desk, the firmness of the chair against my arse and spine so familiar. Countless nights spent dozing in it. The same ashtray of fag butts, some lipstick-stained, some not. Box of matches next to it. The calendar on the wall still stuck on last September, the spare key for the top drawer still taped to the underside of the desk. I go back to that night, sitting here, with Mam dying on her own, vomit on her pillowcase and in her hair, while I looked after Mags' business for a few quid an hour. She didn't even come to the funeral, when I closed the coffin on Mam's gaunt face after spritzing her a few times with her all-important perfume. Didn't even throw an extra fifty my way. Just moaned about having nobody to cover and it being a busy weekend because the Fleadh was on over in Castlebar.

'She's no' here, what do you want?' the older woman is demanding, her dressing gown hanging open to show a faded tattoo on a stretch-marked stomach.

My phone's vibrating in my pocket and I pull it out just as a call ends from Sully. He's sent a text too. I read it, twice. '20 quid win on Mr. Yeats! A fuckin grand! get to Longnecks. Half is yours.' I read it a third time, standing up, kicking myself for not sticking around. For not being beside him as Mr Yeats hopped the last fence, jockey and grandstand roaring him on and the pair of us cheering like wildmen in Ladbrokes, Fat Ray seething behind the till. I don't even realise I'm laughing, punching the air and pacing the room.

'What's funny?' she says, no longer scared, just thinking I'm tapped in the head.

'Myself and a pal had a winner at the horses.'

'So you're here to spend it, or no?' she says, hand on hip, getting fed up.

'And give my money to Mags?' I say, shaking my head, tearing the duct-taped key off the underside of the desk, unlocking the top drawer. Taking out the cash box. At a glance, there's about fifteen hundred in it. I cross the room with the stack of notes and the woman's backing against the wall. I hold it out to her. Fair's fair.

'Take this and you never saw me.'

She meets my eye, almost whispers. 'She'll know.' Her face softens, as if she's calculating the risk, glancing over my shoulder at the can of petrol on the desk, knowing what comes next.

I shake my head. 'There'll be nothing left. There's enough here for you to be long gone by tomorrow.'

She nods. Takes the money then turns and scurries away. I hear them scrambling some things together, then racing away to God knows what den they have to hide in, the young one looking over shoulder and meeting my eye.

I unscrew the canister and pour the petrol across the desk and room. Splash it along the corridors where I know Mags' cameras won't pick me up. One above each bedroom door. One above the front door. None in the office of course, where Mags does her business. None at the back door, where her business partners come and go. Out to the living room, emptying the vodka and whiskey and rum around the place. Back to the office, striking a match and tossing it. Christ, is there a better smell than a freshly struck match? I make sure it takes, none of this walking off with it burning over my shoulder shite you see in films. It catches and the flames stand and stretch and grow and spar and dance.

Then I'm gone, out the back door, hopping the back wall, onto the Racecourse Road, headed for town. Getting Sully on the phone, Mags' bungalow bringing the mercury up a notch or two.

'Story, lad?' I say and he's buzzing about the win. Can hear all the chat in Longnecks in the background. Ask him to call me a pint, tell him I won't be long. Knowing it will be our last big winner around these parts. Knowing that Mags will be out hunting. Knowing that I'm free to run, nothing but open ground in front of me. That I'm the hare now. That I always was. Since I came into this world, ears

and nose twitching, nothing for the likes of me to do but
survive.

The Best Laid Plans

By RT Durant

RT Durant is a widely published author of educational books but has only just turned to fiction. They have completed one novel ('Cruel to be Kind') and a number of stories, one of which 'The Only Time I Ran with the Carving Knife' won a national short story competition. R T Durant is a former secondary school teacher and schools' adviser, who has worked in London, Bristol and Devon.

One August Saturday afternoon a young couple were stumbling along a pine woodland track. There was no wind, and rain was falling in a vertical torrent. The girl was cowering beneath a torn bin liner that shielded her head and formed a shiny cloak down her back. The boy trotted beside her, water steadily oozing into his hair and clothes. They glimpsed the shape of an open woodshed a hundred metres up the track, and they ran and leapt under its cover, squeezing themselves back from the opening. They wriggled out of reach of the drips from the roof, perched on a stack of logs and stared gloomily through the grey-white curtain of rain.

'You didn't need to tear it,' he said at last. She opened out the bin liner that was scrunched up in her fists and inspected it.

'Sorry,' she said. 'I had to. It wasn't big enough to keep me dry.'

He studied her soaked and muddy jeans, her straggly hair. 'It didn't keep you dry anyway.'

'True,' she replied. 'It just seemed the best thing I could do under the circumstances.'

'We needed that bag.'

'I know. Sorry. We'll find something else when we get there.'

'Yes, but anything we take away with us can be traced. It will link us back to the house.'

'Well, it's too late now. We'll just have to improvise. You'll think of something.'

He resented her confidence in him: it implied that he was a co-conspirator, rather than merely a fellow-traveller, a reluctant accomplice. He changed tack.

'But how do you know he'll be out? You said he never goes out.'

She adopted the tone of someone determined to be

patient with a stupid child. 'That's the whole point: this is our only chance. He's being taken out for the day by his cousin's daughter. I know because he was very excited about it last week when I visited him. I'm not just making stuff up as we go along. There's *a plan*.'

He didn't reply.

She dragged her hair to one side and wrung it out, then shook her head vigorously, spraying water droplets in all directions. Now he lost his temper and shoved her off the logs.

'Give over!' he cried. 'And it's not a matter of whether he's going to be in or not; it's just plain wrong what we're planning to do. That's the point, Lottie.'

She picked herself up, brushed herself down pointlessly, and then jabbed the bottom of her heel into the log pile, which gave way, toppling him backwards.

'We've been through this! Do you want to hang around here forever? A levels, university if we're lucky, and then lousy jobs in Mucky Cows' IT department? You're welcome to that life, but *I'm* getting out. No more stepfathers and fake uncles for me. I've had quite enough of those. You stay here, Marcus. I'm sure that fat, sickly sister of yours would be delighted.'

He stayed silent while they resettled themselves on what was left of the log pile. He thought about their normal Saturday afternoons hanging out in her bedroom, smoking, playing cards, making love, holding their breath as they listened to the clink of bottles and singing from downstairs where Lottie's mum revved up for her regular drink-sodden Saturday nights at the Mucky social club. Upstairs and downstairs the routine was familiar – part dangerous, part dull – but reassuring, and he wished he was there now, not squatting in a leaky woodshed, getting ready to rob a 78-year-old man.

'Anyway,' she resumed as though reading his thoughts, 'I'm only robbing

myself. He's never going to use the money, and he said I could have it when he's... when he's... well, you know...no longer here.'

He wouldn't be drawn though. He wasn't going to help her quell her conscience. Everyone knew Lottie as the quiet girl with the heart of gold – the only person willing to give up a couple of hours a week to visit an isolated old man, endure his rambling anecdotes, make him a cup of tea, and do a bit of clearing up. Granted, she was related to him: her mother was the old man's niece, but there were other relatives nearby and none of them felt obliged to visit Jack Crawford more than once a year. Her mother had not seen him in a decade. So that was why when Lottie shared her plan with Marcus as they lay in bed smoking he had been astonished, then intrigued and then excited. Excited because this – to him at least – was a new Lottie, a risky one. It wasn't until he realised he was part of her plan that his enthusiasm subsided a little.

The rain stopped and the sun came out, and they continued down the track to the old man's house which had been erected illegally more than a hundred years ago. Originally nothing more than an elaborate shack, it had grown over the years into a substantial building with a pitched roof and even a cellar – a fait accompli that still offended the local planning office.

Lottie bent down for the key she knew would be under a rock next to the path. Marcus grabbed her arm.

'Hang on. Think. Who else knows about that key?'

'No one. Oh, I see what you mean.'

'Exactly. If there's no sign of a break-in, they'll know that the thief was someone who knew where the key was. You. Us.'

She put the key back and carefully rolled the stone over it.

'So how do we get in?' she asked.

'How would a burglar get in?' He smashed a small window next to the front door, reached in, and undid the latch. She had just stepped into the hallway when Jack Crawford's quivery voice came from the living room.

'Who's that?'

The young couple exchanged shocked glances. Then Lottie rushed into the house.

'It's only me, Uncle. I kept knocking and there was no answer. I was so worried that I smashed a window to get in.'

'I didn't hear. Why didn't you use the key?'

'It wasn't there, Uncle. I looked.'

'Must be there somewhere. Anyway, I told you, you silly girl: I wasn't going to be in today.'

Lottie slapped her hand against her forehead. 'Oh, God, yes, of course. But you are here.' Marcus slipped out, found the key and tossed it into a bush where it would be easy to find.

'I know. Tilly's boy wasn't well, so she had to postpone.'

'Oh well, all's well that ends well. Lucky I forgot you weren't going to be here. Sorry about the window.'

But he didn't mind. Fixing it would give him something to do, and once Lottie had introduced Marcus, and they were sitting together with cups of tea and a plate of elderly custard creams, the old man relaxed, basking in the unexpected presence of the one person whose love he knew he could count on. Before long he had slipped into the well-worn grooves of his favourite monologue – the one which revolved around the idea that while the young are all full of impatient plans for their coming lives when you get old you learn to value not what you might never have, but what you've already got – people, experiences, memories.

'Those are my treasures,' he said, tapping his head sagely. 'All in there. Mind you, you need a few *things* too, reminders. This whole house is a treasure chest of memories: pots, furniture, photos... all reminders of the wonderful life I've had. None of it planned either: it just happened around me.' He fell into a satisfied silence and Lottie caught Marcus's eye and gave him an almost imperceptible nod in the direction of the doorway.

Marcus coughed and rose from his splintered cane chair.

'Er, Mr Crawford, all right if I use the loo?'

''Course. Down the hall.' Marcus briefly narrowed his eyes at Lottie as he left the room. A few seconds later she thought she heard a creak on the stairs.

The old man leaned towards Lottie, lowering his voice in pointless conspiracy. 'You know, you wouldn't believe the things I have kept. I still have all the bus tickets I got when I was a boy. Silly, I know, but the past... the memories that time leaves behind... they're priceless.' He noted the doubt in her expression and was driven on by the urgent need to convince her. 'I know you're in a hurry, Lottie. Desperate for your life to begin, I've no doubt. But don't be in such a rush to let go of your youth. Treasure it.'

'I'm not sure there's much for me to treasure.'

'Ah, you youngsters: you all live in the future. You're all plans, but you're just setting yourself up for disappointment. The thing is to know how to make the most of whatever turns up. No use depending on things turning out how you want them to. The best-laid plans, and all that.' He grinned, desperate to charm her into understanding.

'Schemes.'

'Schemes?'

'It's schemes, not plans. Robert Burns, the poet: he said

that the best-laid *schemes* often go wrong.'

He chuckled, but his reply was cut off by a yell, followed by a series of crashes that ended with loud groaning. While Jack Crawford tried to lever himself out of his chair, Lottie was already in the hallway and staring down into the cellar. She switched on the light and found Marcus lying at the bottom of the steps, jammed up against a large trunk. His eyes were closed but he was still groaning.

'Marcus, what happened?' She slipped her hand beneath his head. He yelled with pain. She looked him over for signs of obvious injury. Round his right ankle, a duvet covers coiled, its remaining material trailing back up the first few stairs. 'Can you get up?' She tried to raise his shoulders.

'No!' he shrieked. 'I'll do it myself. Just stand back, will you?'

He struggled onto his feet, wincing, gasping at every stage of the agonising process. Finally, he stood hunched beneath the glare of the bare bulb, his arms crossed over his body, holding his right side and left shoulder. Lottie helped him back up the stairs and onto the sofa from which the old man had brutally cleared away the jumble accumulated there – catalogues, hats, scarves, mugs, chocolate wrappers – the assorted detritus that congeals round a life of unfettered loneliness.

'I'm so sorry,' he kept repeating. 'I'm such an idiot. I've been warned often enough about those cellar steps and keeping the door locked. Someone was bound to take a tumble before long. I'm amazed I haven't broken my neck going down there.'

After a few minutes, stretched out beneath a dusty blanket, Marcus fell asleep. The old man hovered miserably over him. He knew something should be done, but he didn't know what. He turned, his anguished expression appealing to his great-niece.

'It's alright, Uncle,' she reassured him. 'He'll be okay. Bruised. A bit shocked. And he's got a lot to worry about with his sister and all. A snooze is the best thing for him.'

And the old man was reassured. He didn't want Lottie to grow up, but in truth, there had always been something about her that was wise beyond her years, something she had certainly not got from her mother. She carried with her the sense that everything would turn out all right – even when that was the last thing that could reasonably be expected.

Half an hour later they stood together at the top of the cellar stairs, studying the scene of the disaster, trying to make sense of it.

'I don't know where that duvet cover came from,' the old man mused. 'Looks like the culprit though. Probably tripped over it and before he knew it he was headlong through the door and tumbling down the steps. Poor lad. I feel terrible.'

She put her arm around him and nestled her head against his shoulder.

'Just an accident. It couldn't be helped, and he'll be all right. I don't think he's done any real damage, not to himself. I expect that old trunk came off worse than he did.'

'You know what?' said Jack Crawford as though a sudden decision had come to him, a decision that promised him relief from guilt and worry. 'You can have it right now.'

She pulled away and regarded him in alarm. His face shone with excitement. 'Have what?'

'My treasure. It's no use to me. You can have it. You can take it away with you today. I want you to have it.'

Stunned, unsure how to react, she took refuge in practical matters. 'But how would we carry it? What could we put it all in?'

'You see!' he yelled in triumph. 'You're thinking about

how to make the most of your good fortune. *That's* the way to live. Now, let me see... Come on. We'll get the chest up from the cellar and a solution will come to us.'

As he led Lottie out to the cellar door, she was aware of Marcus sitting up and rubbing the sleep from his face.

'Now,' said the old man. 'I'm sure you and I together can haul that box up the stairs. We'll tie the duvet cover around the trunk handle and then HEAVE!' He was enjoying himself now, and Lottie soon found herself pulling on the make-shift rope with her benefactor until the trunk arrived in the hallway. Marcus had joined them, and despite his pain and the panic on his face, he helped Lottie drag the chest out of the front door and lift it onto an old pram that Jack Crawford miraculously wheeled from around the side of the house.

'There!' the old man cried in triumph. 'I told you: hang onto what you've got because you never really know what you've got until you need it.'

And before they knew it the boy and the girl were wheeling their treasure down the path and back onto the woodland track. They looked back and waved to Jack Crawford, his face the very picture of happiness and foolish youth.

They didn't stop until they reached the wood shelter.

'This is wrong, Lottie. So very wrong. We must take it back now.'

She looked at him mildly, smiling. 'What? It's alright to *steal* his money, but not accept it as a gift?'

'It's all wrong. It was wrong before, and it's wrong now.'

She looked away and sighed. 'You're right of course, but he wants me – us – to have it.' She waited for his response, but he avoided giving one. 'Come on,' she said finally, 'Let's at least take a look.'

She bent down and unfastened the trunk and lifted the

lid. They peered inside. It was full of money, not in neat bundles like in crime films, but in a jumble of ten and twenty-pound notes as though they had been tossed in from time to time. She scooped her hands through the notes, stirring and lifting them to reveal more layers beneath, but as she dug down, the notes became older, larger, and they included unfamiliar colours and denominations. There were green one-pound notes, red ten-shilling notes, and below those, she dug up monopoly money and then hand-drawn notes on yellowing paper. At the bottom, filling nearly half of the trunk were bus tickets, thousands of them, faded but almost every one priced at '4d'. She stopped rummaging through these astonishing contents and stared at Marcus in panic. She turned back to the box and gathered together all the current banknotes. Then she counted them. They amounted to £430. It started raining again.

They sank back onto the dishevelled woodpile in the shelter. After a while, Marcus felt the beginnings of laughter bubbling up from his stomach. He didn't know what was funny. Was it that the old man had played an elaborate joke? But he doubted that there was malice in the old man for that. Was it the old man's touching belief that anyone else would find the trunk's contents valuable? He didn't know, but the laughter finally burst out of him, leavening the pain in his side and his shoulder. Suddenly he felt free; he didn't know what from, but a delicious lightness danced down his legs and set them running, and as he ran, he sensed he was somehow doing exactly what he was meant for. He headed down the track, still laughing, the pain forgotten. After 50 metres he veered to the left and cut a path through the pine trees. She called to him, and he paused, turned. She was standing among the spillings from her uncle's treasure, stray scraps of paper fluttering around her, but although she was looking in his direction, she found nothing to say. He turned again and ran, his heart pumping, and although he didn't know where he was going, he knew that for the first time in his life he was going in the right direction.

A Boy Named Titi

By Tero Tiilikainen

Tero Tiilikainen is a former journalist and a recovering investment banker. His work is minimalist in nature and dialogue driven, with a focus on true-to-life characters that (he hopes) leap off the page. He lives in Dublin, Ireland, with his wife Dawn and his incorrigible dog, Wicket.

Fortune had not been kind to Titi. There was his mom. And the fact that he was stupid. On top of that he was usually hungry.

- You hungry?
- No.
- You sure?

Titi didn't say anything.

- Here. Take half of this.

Our problem was money. We didn't have any.

- You think it will work?
- What do we have to lose?
- What are we talking about?

He was dim. Sure. But not retarded. Don't ever call him retarded. Gus will kill you.

Bam!

- Say it again!
- I won't! I promise!

Kapow!

- I dare you. Say it again!
- I won't! I swear!

Whack!

- You better not.

- What was that about?
- Nothing. Don't worry about it.

Titi knew what it was about. He was smart enough to know that he was stupid.

Titi came bounding around the corner clutching the note.

- She didn't ask any questions?
- No. I just handed her a pencil this time, like you told me to.

Titi passed the note over the counter. Sammy was sympathetic to Titi's mother's plight.

    - *Two* packs today?

Titi nodded. Sammy paused. If Titi was nervous, he didn't show it.

    - That's five fifty, Teee-Tee.

Titi handed over the money and Sammy pulled two packs of Kent Golden Lights from the overhead rack.

    - You tell your mother Sammy say hello.

Titi's mom propped herself up on her elbows with a grunt.

    - Give Mommy her cigarettes.

Titi handed a pack to her.

    - Thank you, baby.

Titi's mom peeled back the cellophane, ripped off the foiled paper, and pulled out her reward.

    - You know, Sammy and me were kind of an item once.

Our first customer was an eighth-grade burnout.

    - I hear you got loosies.

    - Yeah.

    - Gimme two Marlboros.

    - We don't have Marlboros.

    - Parliaments?

    - All we have is Kent Golden Lights.

    - What?

    - Kent Golden Lights. That's all we have.

    - Those are old lady cigarettes.

Gus stayed silent.

    - Fine. Gimme two.

Gus pulled two cigarettes from the pack and handed them over.

    - That'll be fifty cents.

    - Fifty cents? A pack only costs two seventy-five!

- Then go buy a pack.
Our reluctant patron handed over two quarters.

It didn't help that everyone called him Titi.
- It's kind of a stupid name.
- I know.
- Why do they call you it then?
- I dunno.

Twenty loosies at twenty-five cents a pop was five bucks.
Less two seventy-five for new inventory.
That left a profit of two twenty-five.
A Burger King cheeseburger cost ninety-nine cents.
- Two cheeseburgers, please.
We gave them both to Titi and split twenty-seven cents three ways.

Our reputation preceded us on Day Two.
- I'll take one.
- Gimme two.
- Me too!
- We sold out before third period.

Titi came to the door with a bowl of cereal in his hand.
- I can't.
- What? Why?
- She's sleeping.
- It's the middle of the afternoon.
- So?
- So, we need the note!
Gus thought for a moment.
- Take her pack.
- What? No!
- Just take it.

- For what?
- What do you mean for what? Just get the fucking cigarettes.
- Okay.
- But leave the box.
- What?

Gus was a genius.
- What did she say when she woke up?
- Nothing. She thought she smoked the whole pack.
- And?
- And she gave me this.
Titi handed Gus the note. We'd solved our inventory problem.

There were eight of them crammed into that little house. We weren't even sure where they all slept. Titi never invited us inside.

It was a good grift. We were printing money.
- What are you going to buy?
- I don't know. Maybe a bike.
- Me too.
- Yeah, me too. With Tuffs.
- Yeah, Tuffs.
- How many packs do you think we need to sell?

-You back again, Teee-Tee?
- Yeah.
- She need two more packs?
- Yeah.
- That's a lot of cigarettes.
- Yeah.
- You come in last night for two packs. Now you come

again this morning for two more packs?
- Yeah.
- Your mother okay?
- Yeah.
Sammy paused for a moment.
- You tell your mother Sammy say hello.
- I will.
- You know, me and your mother, we used to ... you know.

-You boys need to come with me.
We froze in place.
- Now!
The Vice Principal's office was familiar ground.
- This is a serious offense.
We nodded.
- I'm going to have to call your parents.
We nodded.
- And suspend you for a week.
Gus smirked. I elbowed him in the side.

- What do you guys want to do today?
- I dunno.
- We could go to my house?
- What are we going to do there?
- I dunno.
- We could go to the park.
- For what?
- What do you want to do then?
- I have to buy my mom cigarettes.
- What?
- I have to buy my mom cigarettes.
Titi handed over the note.
- It's in pen.

- Yeah.
- It says two packs.
- Yeah.
- Why?
- She wants in.

Blood Ties

By Ekaterina Crawford

Ekaterina was born and grew up in Moscow and now lives in Aldershot with her husband and their two children. She always loved writing but it's only in the past few years that she really pursued her passion. Ekaterina's creative pieces were published by the Visual Verse Anthology. She has won Writers' Forum Magazine Poetry Competition and was placed 3rd in short stories Competition. She has also won 2021 Kingston Libraries Short Stories Competition.

In anticipation of the afternoon show, the crowds in Kentish Town had already begun to flock towards the concert hall.

'How could you do this to me, David?' Pacing the alley behind the Forum, Liz shouted into her phone. 'No! I don't need another excuse. No! I don't want to know! Allow me to remind you that it was you who begged me to give us another chance. And now another no-show? I can't do this anymore, David. It's over!'

She hung up but a few moments later she dialled back.

'And get your stuff out of my flat! Tomorrow! I have a session in the gym after lunch. Come then. I don't want to see your face ever again!'

Pushing through the concert crowd towards the station, she collided with a tall handsome man dressed way too elegantly for a rock concert. Cursing under her breath, she shot an angry glance at the man, who, stretching his lips in a most charming of smiles, saluted an apology with his umbrella and disappeared into the sea of faces.

Kentish Town station was closed. The white board outside spoke of an earlier passenger incident and members of transport police guided stressed travellers towards the nearest bus stops.

The afternoon was warm. Feeling the need for a dose of fresh air, Liz strolled through Camden and entered Regent's Park via Gloucester Gate.

Reaching the boating lake, she flopped onto the first bench, stretched out her tired legs and began working through her social media accounts, deleting all the evidence of her relationship with David. When she wiped off the last post and changed her relationship status to single, she looked up and saw the familiar four-legged creature trotting towards her from the side the boathouse. The husky dog approached her violently wagging his tail. 'Look who's here!

Hey, buddy!' She scanned the surroundings for the dog's owner. 'Did you run away again?'

The husky danced around her, squealing in excitement.

'Oh, I missed you too!' she laughed, ruffling the dog's thick fur. 'Why can't David be like you? Devoted and loyal?' The dog whined in reply, looking at her with his astonishingly blue eyes. 'Actually, when I think about it, you're kind of the same – both leave me and then both come back when I least expect it. Bad boys! Well, never mind. Come.'

She patted the bench. The dog jumped and curled up next to her, placing his heavy head onto her lap. The husky closed his eyes and lay, not moving, responding to Liz's hand running through his fur with a sound of pure joy, while she, oblivious to what was happening around her, scrolled through the latest headlines.

Gothic nightmare descends upon London.

Blood-drained body found in North-West London.

'Jeez,' she muttered, gently pulling at the husky's ear. 'What is it? The Duke fucking Dracula on the loose?'

'Count,' came from her left.

Liz yelped. Immediately alert, the husky jumped to his feet and growled.

On the bench next to them, sat a young man dressed in a navy-blue suit and tailored black overcoat with a delicate brooch pinned to the lapel. Waves of his dark hair nestled comfortably upon his shoulders. His angular profile was clean and sharp, if a little pale. His strong chin and high cheekbones, together with the slightly elongated nose, seemed strangely elegant and aristocratic. His eyes were hidden behind designer sunglasses. In his hands, he held a black stick umbrella.

Liz stared, restraining the husky with both hands.

'I'm sorry,' the stranger said, removing his shades. His

deep hazelnut eyes gleamed like a liquid gold. 'I didn't mean to startle you. I merely wanted to point out that Dracula was a Count, not a Duke.'

'What? Who cares?' she blurted out. 'Dracula's just a character in a book.'

The stranger smiled, exposing even white teeth.

'Let's leave it to the historians and literati to argue whether Bram Stoker's dramatisation was based on a real person or a fictional character,' he said. Words rolled out of his mouth like water in a stream, soft and smooth. 'Better tell me, what a beautiful lady like you is doing here alone?'

'Can't see how it's any of your business,' Liz retorted, carefully eyeing the stranger. 'Do I know you?'

'My apologies. I didn't mean to pry,' the stranger slightly nodded his head, 'and to answer your question: Yes. We have met. You bumped into me. Earlier today.'

'What?' Liz's hands went limp.

The husky growled, sniffed the stranger, growled again, and climbed onto the bench between them. Leaning against Liz, he pushed the man towards the edge of his seat.

'H-Have you been following me?' Liz glanced around.

'Nothing sinister. I assure you. When I saw you earlier today you seemed…somewhat upset. I simply wanted to make sure you were all right.'

'Oh.' She blushed.

Immune to the stranger's charms, the dog rolled onto its side and pushed harder against the man's leg and then, with his lips stretched and tongue out, looked up at Liz for approval.

'I didn't know people still did that,' she blushed again and patted the husky's belly.

'Did what?' The stranger smiled, amused by the dog's desperate efforts to push him off the bench.

'Cared for what's happening around them.'

'Seemed natural.'

'Not in Central London. Most would've just walked past.'

'I'm glad I didn't.'

He smiled, placed the umbrella on his lap and leaned against the backrest of the bench. The tips of his fingers brushed against Liz's, leaving a hot tingling sensation on her skin. She found herself unable to move, unable to look away. The dog sat up and growled, baring his teeth in warning.

'Sorry,' Liz jerked her head. 'You were saying?'

'I don't think your dog particularly likes me,' the stranger laughed softly.

'He's not mine. He just hangs out with me sometimes. So I guess he feels protective?'

She pulled her hand away and glanced around.

'I'd better be going.'

She got up. The husky jumped off the bench and stood by her feet.

'Thank you for your concern. It was a pleasure to meet you...Tom.'

'Tom?' The stranger raised his perfectly-shaped eyebrow.

With her cheeks turning beetroot once again, Liz pointed at the name sticker attached to the umbrella.

'Oh! This little thing. I...borrowed it. From a person I knew. Allow me to introduce myself. Vladislav Konstantin Alexander Dragan.'

'European?' Liz stared. 'I would never have guessed! Your English is perfect. Where are you from? Italy? Spain?'

'Romania,' he smiled seductively. 'Your tabloids call me "the Romanian Prince".'

'Oh yes, I think I read it somewhere. Wait- Do you mean like a *prince* prince?'

'You could say that,' he smiled again. His eyes glowed softly, reflecting the light of the afternoon sun.

Liz no longer felt like going home. Strangely enough, she was even glad that David had stood her up.

'Elizabeth, Elizabeth Thornton,' she said and stretched out her hand, already imagining herself walking down the aisle of an ancient church with a diamond tiara on her head, and then riding off in a royal carriage. 'Friends call me Liz.'

'Pleasure to make your acquaintance, Miss Thornton,' he placed a gentle kiss on the back of her hand. 'You can call me Vlad. And now, if you'll allow me, I would like to escort you home. It's getting late.'

Vlad led her towards the gates. The husky trotted behind them, keeping a cautious eye on Liz's new acquaintance.

'So. How long are you in London for?' Liz asked as they reached the exit.

'For a couple of weeks,' Vlad said, effortlessly pulling the iron gates open.

'Are you on a royal tour or something?'

Vlad drew her arm through his and pointed his slender finger at the double-decker bus standing at the traffic light.

'"The Week of Romanian Culture in London",' Liz read out loud. 'Right! That explains your reaction when I said Dracula was just a character in a book. He's a part of your country's history!'

Vlad's lips curled.

Behind them, the dog produced a sound transcending from a faint squeal into a low growl.

'So,' Liz prompted, glancing back at her four-legged companion. 'Was he real? The blood-sucking terror?'

'There are a few theories,' Vlad said as they reached the Landmark Hotel. 'We could have discussed it. Over dinner. But I already ate.'

'Yeah, I noticed that!' Liz giggled. 'I'm sorry, I should've said before. You have a little ketchup. There. Allow me.'

He caught her hand before it reached his face, his fingers locked around her wrist like an iron shackle, his hazelnut eyes turned black.

The husky barked. Vlad let go of her hand, pulled a handkerchief from his pocket and wiped the corners of his mouth.

'There,' he said, a familiar golden glow shining through his eyes once again. 'I didn't mean to scare you. It's just... you caught me in a very...um...un-prince-like moment. I apologise. Humbly. And to make it up to you, if you'll allow it, of course, I'd like to buy you a drink.'

In the Bell Inn, they ordered drinks and took a table by the back wall. Outside, the husky barked and squealed, begging to be let in. Each time the door opened, Liz stole a quick glance of the furry creature that sat patiently by the front door, sniffing each new visitor entering the pub.

'That dog seems very attached to you,' Vlad said, placing a bottle of tequila, saltshaker, and a plate with lemons on the table.

'He's been following me around for some months now. He comes and goes. I don't even know whose he is.'

'Well, doesn't matter.' Vlad poured out a shot of tequila and pushed it closer to Liz. 'Better tell me what made you so upset?'

'I had a fight with my boyfriend.' Liz downed the shot and bit into a lemon wedge. 'Ah, that's good! Not boyfriend, more of a fiancé really. Well, ex-fiancé turned boyfriend again, ex-boyfriend now...I guess.'

'Sounds complicated.' Vlad refilled her glass.

'Not really. Well, yes it was. In a way. Not anymore.'

'I'm sorry to hear it.'

His hand covered hers; the light tingling sensation spread over her skin.

'It's all right. It was long coming. We drifted apart about

a year ago. He asked me to give it another chance. I made an effort. He made promises...You know how it is.'

'I'm afraid I don't,' Vlad shook his head. 'I would never have betrayed my word to such a beautiful lady like yourself.'

Liz smiled, drowning in his dark eyes.

'You know what?' she said after downing another shot. 'It's getting late, and I was thinking, do you, maybe, want to come over to my place? I live just around the corner. We can have a quiet drink. Or two. Get to know each other a little better.'

'You just broke up with your boyfriend. I don't want–' his fingers caressed her cheek.

'Don't worry, you won't take advantage of my broken heart. Whatever happens, happens. No strings attached.'

'If you insist.' He leaned in, his cold lips brushed lightly against hers. 'Just give me a minute.'

Vlad got up and strolled off towards the toilets.

With nothing else to do, Liz turned her attention to the news feed on the large TV that hung behind the bar. The screen showed a police cordon and a coroner's van. The breaking news message at the bottom of the screen read:

The body found earlier today in Kentish Town has now been officially identified as 29-year-old Tom Mitchel from Hampstead Heath. Police appealing for any witnesses.

Liz stared at the TV screen, then at the umbrella perched against the wall, then at the screen again, and then at the untouched glass of red wine on the table in front of her.

The vision of her royal wedding faded away, replaced by the sight of a police cordon and a coroner's van.

Immediately sober, she grabbed her bag and rushed out of the pub. Hiding behind the delivery van and keeping her eyes on the front door, she slowly backed off until she slipped and landed into the puddle of dark sticky substance next to the bloodless corpse dressed in the UPS uniform.

Slipping and slithering, she scrambled up to her feet and dashed to the other side of the deserted street. She ran into the churchyard and hid behind a headstone. The full moon shed its cold silver onto the graves. Somewhere in the distance, a dog howled.

'You can run, but you can't hide,' Vlad's deep voice came from the other side of the churchyard.

Covering her mouth with both hands, Liz froze. She closed her eyes, trying to blend into the headstone. Blood throbbed in her temples, echoing approaching steps.

'Hello, beautiful,' Vlad whispered into her ear.

She spun around, her horrified eyes met his black stare.

'Now. How about that drink?' he smiled, his canine teeth grew longer.

An ear-piercing scream ripped through the air. She couldn't recognise her own voice. Vlad yanked her up as if she was no heavier than a rag doll and threw her to the other side of the yard.

Liz landed hard, hitting her face against the stone wall. Her vision began to blur, surroundings slowly fading away. Now it was only her and a slowly approaching dark shadow. Its sinister laugh rang in her ears.

She opened her eyes. Vlad's white, luminous skin looked almost transparent against the backdrop of the night sky. His cold fingers touched the cut on her face.

'It would be a pity to kill you,' he said licking the blood off his fingers. 'But you're so delicious.'

Vlad grabbed the sides of her jacket, pinned her against the wall and drew back the collar of her blouse, exposing her jugular vein.

'Goodbye, Liz Thornton. It was a pleasure to make your acquaintance.'

Resigned to her fate, Liz went limp in his hands. But just

before the sharp teeth sunk into her skin, she saw a flash of silver fur as the husky charged at the vampire, pushing it away.

The dog stood between her and Vlad. Then with a menacing growl, he launched forward, knocking the vampire off its feet. The churchyard became loud with heavy grunts and barks. The two predators growled and snarled, snapping their teeth, trying to get a taste of each other's flesh.

The husky was the first to succeed. Vlad roared in pain, shook the dog off his leg, and kicked it hard, sending it flying to the other side of the yard. With a cry of pain, the dog crashed into a gravestone. Then everything went quiet. The vampire vanished, leaving its prey behind.

Liz found the husky by one of the graves. He was lying still, his belly rising and falling with each laboured breath.

'Come on, buddy,' she sobbed, stroking his fur. 'Get up. Please.'

The dog opened his eyes, pressed his nose against her hand, and closed them again. On his head, just above his eye, a deep wound oozed blood.

Liz carefully heaved the dog off the ground and carried it to her apartment.

After attending to the Husky's wounds, she left him on the couch. She showered, changed into a clean tracksuit, and made herself strong coffee with a shot of whisky. Curled on the sofa next to her four-legged saviour, she stared at the large silver disk of the moon that hung outside her window.

The next morning, she woke up in her own bed.

Staggering into the empty lounge, she heaved herself onto the sofa and clasped her head between her palms, trying to silence the toll of the hangover bells. Did she dream it all? Vampires? Dead bodies? A nearly finished bottle of whisky on the floor by the couch confirmed her suspicions.

Wrapped in the duvet, ready to give in to a hungover slumber, she heard the sound of a boiling kettle, which was followed by the smell of freshly brewed coffee coming from the kitchen.

'David?' Liz scrambled up to her feet, and with a duvet still upon her head, waddled into the kitchen. 'What the fuck, David? I thought I told you I don't want to...'

She froze in the doorway. David stood by the table. His shirt was undone, revealing a huge bruise on the left side of his torso. There were a few small scratches across his face and a deep cut on the left side of his temple, just above his eye.

'Morning love,' he smiled, his astonishingly blue eyes gleamed in the light of the morning sun. 'Thank you for looking after me yesterday. I hope that bloodsucker didn't scare you too much. Coffee?'

'You?' Liz muttered, the duvet slowly sliding onto the floor. 'You! It was you all the time!'

She took a cautious step closer and ran her fingers over the scarring skin above his eye. David drew back.

'Careful, love. I heal fast, but it still hurts like hell.'

'W-why didn't you tell me?'

'Would you have believed me if I did?' he smiled.

'No way!' she brushed off approaching tears and buried her face into his chest. 'Though it does explain why you've refused to adopt a cat.'

David chuckled, placing a soft kiss upon her head. 'I always told you, I'm more of a dog person.'

Peccadilloes

By Thomas de la Mare

Thomas 'Tom' de la Mare developed an interest in books and reading at such a young age that he has no recollection of doing so. At 27, he now lives in Dorset with his fiancée and his dog, both of whom live in fear that his ever-growing collection of books will eventually render the house uninhabitable. He writes in the blissful moments of equilibrium after inspiration has struck and procrastination dwindled.

In the average life span – currently estimated to be 72.6 years – a person experiences 26,499 days. They experience them, yet they do not necessarily *live* them. Of these 26,499, something like 1,500 can be omitted as forgotten due to infancy. A further few hundred due to ill health, drunkenness or some kind of drug-addled stupor. The vast majority of the remainder can be expunged from our little data set because they are in no way memorable. Given the undoubted blessing of such an opportunity, were a man or woman of exactly 72.6 years of age ruminating on their days spent up until such a point, they would be hard-pressed to remember more than a few hundred. If one chose to be particularly limiting in how we define 'remember' here, the argument could be made that you don't actually *remember* – in the sense that you could recount more than 70 per cent of what happened on said day – more than a handful of days. Your wedding, the birth of your first-born, the death of your mother; maybe yesterday and the day before, due only to their recency. Everything else, were you asked to recount your exact movements in the interests of a narrative, to satisfy a jury, or purely because somebody quite nicely asked you to do so, would be resigned to a few highlights of a day at best. These assertions are true for, what I will beg forgiveness for terming them as such, 'normal people'.

Now 'normal' versus 'unusual' is a linguistic distinction that, like so many others in the modern world, comes under increasing fire for its applicability in recent years. 'Normal' implies that something is correct, that it fits in, or that, bluntly, it's good. 'Unusual' implies an imperfection, something that sticks out for some reason, or that, equally bluntly, is bad. You will note my use of the word 'imply', rather than the word 'infer'. When faced with an overwhelming desire, compulsion or choice – motivated

by any number of factors one can think of – to ignore the
context of a situation, the above conclusions as to the
intentions behind 'normal' and 'unusual' are perhaps valid.
In others, it becomes clear that 'normal' merely means
an expected outcome, or something that the majority of
things conform to. In the above use of the word 'normal',
the intent was merely to refer to people who haven't either
been, seen someone be, or heard about someone else being,
shot in the head.

Jim Reed lived a relatively ordinary life – there is no
time to go into the relative merits of the term 'ordinary'
here and compare its contextualisation, just interpret it
however you want. Jim was in his early thirties, worked
as an analyst for a medium-sized company, lived with his
ordinary wife and his ordinary children in an ordinary
house in Dorset. Ordinary. Of an evening, Jim enjoyed
browsing various 'news' sites (we really won't go into what
can be considered 'news' here as we've all got lives to get on
with) and then posting his views on various items he may
find on his Twitter account, 'JimmyR1990'. JimmyR1990
had 310 followers, but due to the public nature of his
profile, far more than 310 people saw a three-tweet diatribe
on vaccinations that Jim posted one Tuesday. A diatribe
which admonished the vaccinated as 'sheep', and the
vaccines as autism- and cancer-causing monstrosities.
The fact that Jim himself was vaccinated as a child, with
the MMR vaccine being introduced in 1988 is, of course,
immaterial to such a righteous condemnation as that
which was launched into cyberspace from the virtual pen of
JimmyR1990.

About 30 miles away from the launchpad of Jim, a man
named F Linus was one of these more than 310 people who
saw Jim's tweets. After reading said tweets, Mr Linus next
took to viewing Jim's Facebook profile, then his LinkedIn,

then a recent fundraising page that Jim was involved in that listed his home address at the bottom. Mr Linus briefly considered referring the conduct of Jim to his manager at the medium-sized company he worked at. Briefly. What Mr Linus actually did was print off a photo of Jim and write down his address in a small notebook titled 'Peccadilloes', alongside a summarised version of Jim's tweet. He then slipped this notebook alongside something equally small, but metallic and of a less uniform shape, into the pocket of his coat before stepping outside his front door.

Jim Reed's house was back from a relatively quiet road, accessed through a gate that led on to a long pathway up to his front door. Every year around September when the darkness of a day began to outweigh the light, the thought occurred to Jim that he should put some kind of security light on the front of this house. That way, not only could he be alerted by someone walking up the pathway, but he also greatly reduced the risk of him or one of his family tripping up on one of the five steps that featured on said path in the darkness. It is difficult to tell if Jim's life would have been saved had this occurrence of thought ever progressed into tangible action; but seeing as it didn't ever progress that far, it seems wasteful to dwell on it. Mr F Linus approached Jim's house just after seven o'clock one evening, having watched his routine for the three days prior. Jim returned at around five o'clock from work, and at around half past six each night, Jim's wife and his two children departed to what Mr Linus assumed was some kind of children's club or sporting activity. It hardly mattered. They didn't return until eight o'clock, and nobody left the house again until the following morning. Mr Linus was therefore comfortable that Jim was still in at just after seven that particular evening, and that he was alone. Mr Linus strode purposefully along the pathway, effortlessly accounting for the five steps, before knocking resoundingly on the door.

Despite the lack of a security light, what Jim did have was a small peep hole in his front door. A peep hole that he saw fit to use whenever somebody called uninvited, especially when it was dark. Jim's brow knitted itself together momentarily at the knock, but he quickly crossed his front room having got up from where he sat, walked down the hall and squatted to squint through the peep hole, given that it was only about five feet up the front door. The bullet that came through that same peep hole tore through Jim's right eye, barrelled through his brain and the back of his skull before exiting with a firework-esque bloom of blood and brain matter, and driving itself into the plaster of the hallway behind Jim's head. There was the staccato, echoing noise of a blood splatter falling onto a hardwood floor before a dull, almost anticlimactic, thud of Jim's body hitting the very same. And that was the end of Jim Reed.

F Linus tucked his pistol back inside his coat, taking a small piece of paper out of the other pocket and sliding it discreetly through the letterbox. He would be long gone before Jim's wife returned home with her two children to find the rapidly stiffening body of her husband laying in what one could be forgiven for thinking appeared to be a peaceful sleep, were there not a ragged, bloody hole in his face where his right eye had been, and a pool of crimson around his head. At his feet lay a small piece of paper, a pure square of white blemished by only nine words in an elaborate cursive:

Useless are the Eyes when the Thoughts are Blind

Rebecca Adams was, if I may permitted to use the term yet again, an ordinary person. She was five feet six inches tall, with mousy brown hair, and a face that performed those tasks expected of a face entirely admirably. Rebecca, or Becky to those who knew her, lived alone in a ground-floor flat in Bournemouth. Much like our friend Jim, whom she never met yet shared such a significant life event with, she worked for a medium-sized company doing a job that any successful creative will tell you to quit immediately to follow your dreams and not be a dull member of the 'machine', but any rational human being will tell you is merely the standard lot in life for the vast majority of humanity. A job that, in other words, was ordinary.

Becky – I think we know her well enough to use the nickname by now – liked to spend her weekends out and about with one of several cadres, be it her school friends, university friends, or work friends. On one such weekend, during the heady days of the summer of 2020 when the British population was temporarily free once more to set about infecting each other with the COVID-19 disease as much as they pleased, safe in the knowledge that under no circumstances would they ever return to the lockdowns of the spring, Becky made a mistake. A rather costly mistake.

Conversation had turned to the prospect of the possibility of a vaccine for the coronavirus, a presumed solution to the ongoing pandemic that Becky and all of her friends were firmly behind. In fact, fuelled by the fourth of the seven drinks Becky would imbibe that evening, she saw fit to brand anyone who didn't immediately and willingly get the vaccine as soon as it was offered a 'fucking idiot' and deserving of the kind of slow, unpleasant death those afflicted with coronavirus endured. As one enamoured with such a conviction and buoyed by the intoxication of alcohol is wont to do, Becky uttered these words in what it would be fair to term, not her 'inside voice'. Unfortunately, at least from Becky's perspective, there was someone inside with her when she used said voice, someone who, given the choice, she would rather had not heard her.

Mr F Linus raised his eyebrows in a mixture of surprise and resignation, the look of one who has settled on a now unavoidable course of action. He flipped open his notebook, still entitled 'Peccadilloes', and wrote out a short description of the woman across the bar who had just made her feelings on anti-vaxxers abundantly clear, noting down a shorthand version of what she had done to warrant taking up a page in his book. He felt entirely confident he could follow this woman home without any trouble, but it never hurt to be doubly sure in such circumstances. He sighed, closing his notebook carefully and taking another sip from the glass of iced water which sat in front of him. That same glass remained equally full when Becky departed the bar not ten minutes later.

F Linus gazed through the window at Becky, his eyes half closed in the hooded expression of one mired in apathy. He had followed Becky to two further bars, before following her home in a cab – Linus continued to be surprised at how many taxi drivers will take the instruction 'follow that cab' with little to no questioning – and now he was outside her flat. Becky had put a pizza in the oven, before promptly falling asleep or perhaps passing out on the sofa. Linus crouched slightly, closing his left eye as he gazed down the sights of his pistol with right. The shot he took was measured, calculated and accurate. It entered Becky's head just above her left eye, and she was dead before the bullet embedded itself in the sofa cushion behind her head. A thin stream of blood dribbled from the wound, down the side of her nose, to congeal on her lip. It would be nearly two days before somebody came round to check on her. Once they'd finished screaming and called the police, the door was kicked in to reveal a small white piece of paper on the floor. A small piece of paper which read:

Useless are the Eyes when the Thoughts are Blind

Confession

By Susan Martin

Susan Martin is a retired secondary school teacher, who is fortunate to have been able to retire a little early to enjoy life and to have time for her interests. She plans to write more now she has the time – poems and stories. She lives in Port Talbot, South Wales, with her husband, their Westie, and their three cats. She also enjoys walking, photography, reading, sewing and knitting.

The day I discovered my husband killed Megan, I was sitting opposite him drinking coffee. It was cheap coffee, bitter and burnt. An oily film from the UHT milk floated on the top of the brown liquid. Only the sugar, two sachets of granulated white sweetness, made it drinkable. Just.

I shifted uncomfortably on the hard plastic chair and pulled my sweatshirt sleeves down so they covered my thin, pale wrists. Around us, the hum of other people's conversations was punctuated by the cry of a frustrated child and the cough of a stale lung.

It was a far cry from our first date in Cardiff, twelve years ago. We had drunk rich creamy cappuccinos then, as we tried to decide whether this was a quick coffee, a night of passion, a casual few weeks or something serious. I knew by the end of the date that Will was no placeholder. Eighteen months later, we were married in a small chapel by the sea in his native Pembrokeshire.

'Hey,' he roused me from my memories. His dark brown eyes met mine and he nodded slightly as if asking for confirmation that I was listening.

'Sorry, I was miles… years… away. Look, Will, why are you here? Why are we meeting?' I asked.

'I want a reconciliation,' he stated. His broad mouth grinned at me and he reached for my hand. Quickly, I pulled my hand away. No touching. That was the rule.

'Yeah, funny… Look, I don't have time for this.' I did. I had nothing better to do. And, to be honest, I had looked forward to this day for weeks, to seeing him, to hearing his deep, warm voice. 'What do you really want?'

He told me he wanted to tell me about Megan. I sighed. I really didn't want to listen to him tell me again how sorry he was, but they couldn't help themselves, and she was so special, such a beautiful spirit. But I had to. I knew that. So I nodded and prepared myself to stifle my jealousy, my disappointment, my anger.

'I killed her,' he said.

'What?'

That was far too loud for where we were. A few smirking faces turned towards us. A member of staff raised her chin in query. Was everything all right? I nodded.

Will hushed my startled outcry with a gesture and leaned forward. 'I killed her.'

It took a few seconds for me to process this information. To decide how to respond. I had known, deep down, that he'd killed her, ever since I'd heard, on BBC Wales News, about the discovery of her body in the neat living room of her small terraced valley home. No jumping up in surprise and spilling my large glass of wine when the newsreader, with her practised soulful look, described the tragic death that had shocked neighbours.

I'd known about their affair too.

'Why?' I asked simply.

Will shrugged. 'Pressure. She wanted me to divorce you and marry her.' Will could never deal with pressure. He had inveigled his way into becoming the captain of the Sunday league football team he played for. Two weeks – no, not quite that even – and he had resigned the role claiming, rather arrogantly I thought to myself, that friendship and football were more important to him than being a leader.

'Why didn't you just finish with her?' Or leave me? It struck me for the first time that I could have been the body found strangled and sprawled over the sofa. So, I was lucky. However, it really hadn't felt like that during the last few months.

'I tried, honestly.' His chestnut-brown eyes beseeched me to believe him, just like he'd pleaded with me to believe he wasn't sleeping with her, wasn't in love with her, wouldn't leave me. 'But she wouldn't accept it. She kept calling me. She sent dozens of texts – every day. She even turned up at my work, Jess.' He shrugged again. What could he do, he wanted me to agree.

He'd always looked to me for agreement, for confirmation, for acceptance. When he'd insulted my dad at our wedding, when he'd cancelled our anniversary break so he could play golf, and when he'd forgotten to turn up for my niece's christening. And I'd given him that confirmation that it was all right, that I understood, that it wasn't his fault. What a loved-up idiot I had been. And, no doubt, Megan had been taken in too.

I had no sympathy for Megan, though. She'd made it clear to me from the day we met that she fancied Will and nothing was going to stand in her way. She'd been staying with her sister, Cora, our neighbour, following the break-up of a relationship, and suddenly she was part of our circle. She'd be at the local pub, walking her sister's dog in the park, at the birthday barbecue a few houses down.

I could see Will was enchanted. I understood. She was beautiful. Long red curls bounced, her plump breasts bounced, she bounced in excitement every time Will made a joke. After nearly ten years of marriage, he was more than ready for an affair. And that was all the encouragement Megan had needed.

Before he left, before I drove him away with my possessiveness, he claimed, I warned Megan off. Stupid? Reckless? Dangerous as it turned out.

By then, she'd moved into her own house and I took flowers as a moving in gift. Gladioli symbolise faithfulness and honour. The subtlety was lost on Megan. In any case, they were an excuse, of course, to speak to her. I was reasonable at first, but she laughed in my face. Her small, perfect, white teeth sprung apart and her fleshy sword of a tongue curled in delight. If I had to beg another woman to leave my husband alone then he was no longer my husband, not emotionally, she'd argued. I was pathetic. I was needy. No wonder Will didn't want me any more.

It ended when Cora, her sister, let herself in with her key. Tears chasing down my cheeks, I was bundled out onto the street, to the amusement of the next-door neighbour, who was still wearing pink polka-dot pyjamas at noon, and who had clearly heard our row through the thin walls. This time, I was warned off.

Cora appreciated how I felt – she didn't – but I couldn't harass her sister. That's life, Cora counselled me. I had to get over it, move on. I wanted to spit at her, to hiss that her sister was a bitch but I just gulped back my angry tears and nodded and complied when she suggested I go home.

And it was that visit, that curious neighbour, of course, that had helped seal my fate. I had had a screaming row with Megan two days before she died. Before she was killed. Prime suspect.

'You told the police you suspected me,' I said. The detective sergeant, barely able to contain her delight that this case would be solved so quickly, had told me that Will hadn't wanted to tell them, that they had really had to drag the information out of him. Even then, in that squat, grey interview room, I had doubted that. He loved Megan, I thought, and, if he believed I had killed her, he would want me punished.

He shrugged again and it was all I could do to resist the urge to reach across the table and slap him. But that would spoil everything. I had to remain calm, stay seated, not touch him.

'Why?' I demanded. 'To lead the police away from you?'

'Hmm... maybe. But look, divorce is expensive, messy. This way I've got Megan and you out of my hair.' His shoulders lifted slightly and his palms spread apart to indicate that I should understand. What else could he do?

For a moment I was truly speechless. This time I would not give him the agreement, the confirmation, the acceptance he always craved. He was prepared to see me rot in this heart-breaking, spirit-destroying jail, rather than go through the expense and inconvenience of a divorce. How had I ever loved this man?

I shook my head, trying to get my thoughts together. My heart was pounding now. I had one more question I had to ask.

'Why are you telling me this?'

'So when you're locked up in your cell, you have something to think about. The favour you did me.' He grinned as my mouth fell open at his cruelty. 'Anyway, I've got to go soon; I've got a date. So many women are sympathetic to a man in my situation.' He winked at me.

I had heard enough. I got up and without a word walked towards the bored, grey prison officer at the door. Unable to resist a final glance at Will, I turned, only to see him shrug once more before standing up.

The prison officer pressed the buzzer and accompanied me through the door, out of the visiting area, and into the corridor.

'In here,' she instructed and I went into the office. Leaning on the grey metal desk, I reached under my prison-issue sweatshirt, removed the listening device that had been attached to me, and handed it to the prison officer.

She pointed to one of the monitors. I smiled as I saw Detective Sergeant Cleverly apprehend Will just as he approached the prison exit.

Bogeyman

By Ekaterina Crawford

Ekaterina was born and grew up in Moscow and now lives in Aldershot with her husband and their two children. She always loved writing but it's only in the past few years that she really pursued her passion. Ekaterina's creative pieces were published by the Visual Verse Anthology. She has won Writers' Forum Magazine Poetry Competition and was placed 3rd in short stories Competition. She has also won 2021 Kingston Libraries Short Stories Competition.

Wrestled out of a hot and sweaty
dream, with my mouth still full
of its salty taste, I stare into
the dark corner of my childhood room,

wide-eyed, as the shadows
begin their ritual dance. Lurking,
at the back of my room,
of my mind, they had lain in wait,

but now flooding in –
repressed memories of the past.
Your dark shadow in the dim
moving closer. Closer. Reaching,

where's sacred, your stale breath
fills the air and scalds my face.
On the bed, like on the altar, virgin's
sacrificed for blood, rough hands

touch where it's forbidden,
innocence nipped in the bud.
Thirty-odd years since, I remember
you only had to die to spur

the memories, of what had happened
of the evil monster that you were.
The coffin moves into the cremator,
and mother sobs squeezing my hand.

As you're engulfed and turn to ashes,
I pray to God, you burn in hell.

Printed in Great Britain
by Amazon